DANNY PEARSON WILL RETURN

For updates about current and upcoming releases, as well as exclusive promotions, visit the authors website at:

www.stephentaylorbooks.com

Also by Stephen Taylor
The Danny Pearson Thriller Series

Snipe
Heavy Traffic
The Timekeepers Box
The Book Signing
Vodka Over London Ice
Execution Of Faith
Who Holds The Power
Alive Until I Die
Sport of Kings
Blood Runs Deep
Command to Kill
No Upper Limit
Leave Nothing To Chance

No
Upper
Limit

Stephen Taylor

1

Director of Operations for Greenwood Security, Danny
Pearson was packing up for an early finish. He turned
his PC off and shouted goodbye to his boss and close
friend Paul Greenwood before heading for the exit. As
he passed the front desk, Angela waved him to a halt.

'Mr Pearson, there's a lady waiting to see you,' she
said, pointing to an attractive young lady sitting in
reception.

'Right, er, ok, thank you, Angela,' Danny said,
checking his watch as he turned to give the woman a
warm smile. 'How can I help you, Mrs... ?'

'Miss, actually. Amanda Wallace,' she said with the
directness of somebody used to getting their own way.

'How can I help you, Miss Wallace?'

'I'm a journalist and I'm doing a story on an arms
dealer called the Wolf. My father, David Wallace, was a
journalist following the activities of the Wolf back in
Afghanistan. Unfortunately, the Wolf killed him when

he got too close to discovering his identity.'

'I'm sorry, Miss Wallace, but I'm really pushed for time and I don't see what this has to do with me,' Danny said, slightly perturbed by the woman's directness. Danny was fully aware of the Wolf and his activities. He'd been sent on missions to catch him back in his SAS days. He also recognised the name David Wallace, the memory of him and his unit trying to keep the man alive until a helicopter could evacuate them, replaying vividly in his head.

'A camera and notebook were amongst my father's possessions, they contained pictures of you and your SAS unit, and a picture of the Wolf from the day he died. Look, I'm close to finding out who he is. I just want to make him pay for what he did to my father,' she said, speaking fast, a cold determination in her voice.

Danny's face turned hard as stone. He leant in and spoke quietly but firmly to her. 'I'm afraid I can't help you, Miss Wallace. I can't talk about any activity relating to my days in active service. My unit's anonymity and safety are of paramount importance. I strongly advise you to destroy those photos and forget you ever saw them.'

'I'm not here to cause you any trouble. I'm just trying to get justice for my father,' she replied, her tone softening as she tried to play on his emotions.

'I can't help you,' was all Danny said in return.

'Just think about it. Here, take my number. If you change your mind, call me,' she said, pushing a business card at him.

'I won't,' Danny said, taking it and shoving it in his jeans pocket before walking out the office door.

Paul Greenwood watched curiously from the other side of the office, turning back into his office after Danny left, closely followed by Miss Wallace.

***

On the street below, two men in a Ford Transit van watched as Danny's BMW came out from the underground car park and headed off down the road. Minutes later, Amanda Wallace exited the foyer doors and flagged down a taxi. The driver of the van spun it around in the road to follow the taxi while his passenger pressed the call button on his mobile.

'We're too late. She went to see Soldier Boy before we could get to her,' the passenger said in an Eastern European accent.

'It's ok, everyone is in place, we'll just have to deal with them all in one go. Where's the woman now?'

'She got in a taxi. We're following it.'

'As soon as she's alone, get the photos and notebook, then kill her.'

He hung up. The van settled in two cars back from the taxi. They followed it towards London's West End until it pulled into a taxi lane and started pulling away.

'Just keep following,' the passenger said to the driver.

They moved the van into the taxi lane and continued to follow, cruising past the stationary traffic to their right, ignoring the occasional honk of a horn from angry commuters, road raged by them cutting the queue.

A hundred metres further up they undertook a police car which immediately put its siren and lights on, pulling into the taxi lane in pursuit.

'We'll have to pull over,' said the driver, as they had no chance of losing them in the van.

'Shit, give me your gun,' said the guy in the passenger seat, putting his and the driver's handguns in the glove box out of sight before punching the dash in frustration as the taxi drifted away, turning off out of sight as they pulled to a halt.

They stopped and wound down the window as the police officer walked up to the driver's side.

'A relation to Lewis Hamilton, are we, sir?' the officer said with dry sarcasm.

2

Turning onto his street, Danny parked outside his three bed terraced house in Walthamstow. It was only five o'clock, but being the middle of winter, the sun had long since set. He got out and locked the car, shivering a little as he headed up the path towards his front door. An uneasy feeling made him stop short of the door and turn. He didn't move for what seemed like an age, a cloud of vapour escaping his mouth in the frosty night air. His eyes darted across every detail on the street, trying to figure out what had put his senses on edge. There was nothing he could put his finger on, no suspicious people, no sinister vehicles with blacked-out windows, nobody he didn't recognise looking out of neighbours' windows. Satisfied but still on edge, he turned back, popped the key in the lock, and entered the house. His phone rang as he closed the door, causing him to answer it before turning the hall light on.

'Hello.'

'Code red, brother, wherever you are, get out, get out now! I'm with Chaz, I haven't got hold of Smudge yet. Get out and meet us at the place. I'll explain there.'

'Roger that,' Danny said, hanging up on his friend and previous SAS team member, Fergus McKinsey.

Sliding the phone back in his pocket, Danny left the hall light off and stood stock still, his eyes acclimatising to the orange glow of the streetlight through the stained glass window pane in the front door. He slowed his breathing and concentrated on the sounds of the house, tuning out the tick of the central heating system and the faint hum of the fridge freezer. Danny stood there in an almost trancelike state for nearly five minutes.

There you are.

The house was old with original floorboards. The faintest creak emanated from the kitchen as someone's weight shifted. Sliding a hand into the umbrella stand, he lifted his old baseball bat straight up and out, taking care not to touch the sides and make a noise.

***

Standing silently in the dark kitchen, the source of the noise fought to keep his nerves in check. He blinked away a trickle of sweat. His face was hot and itchy in the balaclava. The target had entered the house, followed by silence. The standoff was causing his muscles to scream as he stood tensed up. His silenced Sig P365 was held up on extended arms, pointing at the doorway leading to the hall. Eventually, the lactic acid built up beyond containment and he had to move to relieve his discomfort. Seconds later, the click of the living room light switch echoed in the silence, followed by a newsreader's voice coming from a TV.

Thankful to be moving, he flattened himself beside the entrance to the hall. Dressed entirely in black, he was visible only as an ominous shadow in the dark. He took a quick glance down the hall, sliding his body through at the sight of the flicking, pulsating light emanating from the TV in the lounge. Moving silently, rolling his trainers heel to toe, he edged to the entrance to the living room. With his adrenaline and confidence growing, he spun in and popped two bullets centre mass into a shadowy figure sitting on the sofa. In the second it took him to realise it was just a coat laid over the back of the seat, Danny exploded out of the downstairs toilet behind him. His face lit up by the TV in a terrifying mask of fury and menace. The baseball bat powering down onto the man's wrist, knocking the gun into the shadows as it fractured bones. Shock kept the man pain free and panicked self preservation kept him moving as Danny came in for another swing. He ducked just in time, the bat brushing his hair as it passed overhead, embedding itself into the TV screen with a flash and puff of smoke, plunging the room into darkness. Swinging his body weight into a left hook, he powered his good fist into Danny's ribs, knocking him sideways. Springing away from Danny, he pulled a serrated commando knife out of a sheath on the back of his belt.

Danny straightened himself up, the baseball bat held with two hands, knuckles white as he gripped tightly.

The two men stood circling each other in the faint orange glow coming through the curtains from the streetlights outside. Darting forward as if to attack, Danny forced the man in the balaclava to lunge at him with the knife. Dodging it, Danny went low, swinging the bat with all his might into the side of the man's knee, wrecking the joint and folding his leg into an unnatural angle as he dropped to the floor screaming. Moving forward, Danny towered over him, treading on the wrist of his knife hand and pushing the end of the baseball bat into the man's throat until he let go of the knife.

'Who sent you?' he growled.

'Fuck you,' the man spat back through the choking and pain, his accent unmistakably Eastern European.

Quick as lightning, Danny pulled the bat from his neck and cracked it on the side of his busted knee. He waited for the man to stop screaming and writhing in pain before pushing the bat back on his throat.

'Who sent you?' he said again, his voice calmer this time.

'I don't know. Kovak paid me to kill you.'

'Who's Kovak?' Danny said, jerking the bat ready for another blow.

'Kovak, he's a drug dealer, works for a big player called Anton. That's all I know,' the man said, stammering through the pain.

Danny looked around in the orange glow. The gun under the sofa caught his eye. Throwing the bat to one side, he knelt on the man's chest and reached across to grab it, pulling a cushion off the sofa with the other hand. He pushed it over the man's face, covering his eyes as they went wide through the balaclava. Pushing the silencer into the soft pillow, Danny pulled the trigger twice. The body jerked, then lost all tension, leaving Danny in the orange glow in silence.

3

After a few seconds, Danny kicked himself into action. He patted the body down. There was no ID or wallet, as expected. He found two spare magazines, a burner phone and a folded sheet of paper with a picture of him and his old SAS unit on it. Shoving them into his jacket pocket, Danny ran upstairs, leaving the lights off as he went into the bedroom. Sliding to his knees by the built-in wardrobe, Danny slid the door open and threw his shoes out behind him. Grabbing a prepacked old army backpack, he pulled it out and placed it beside him. Hooking a finger in a hole in the corner of the wardrobe's base, Danny pulled it up and rested it against the wall. He grabbed two bundles of cash sealed in freezer bags and shoved them into the backpack along with a selection of passports and pay as you go phones. Sliding his jacket off, he pulled out two Glock 17 handguns already in a double shoulder holster and put them on. Lastly, he put a box of ten full magazines into the backpack.

As he slid his jacket back on, a neighbour's dog barking outside caused him to turn his head. He scurried over to the window on his knees, moving up in the dark until he could see out. Three figures, dressed in black jackets, jeans and out of place, different coloured trainers moved towards the front door carrying MP5 submachine guns in white latex-gloved hands, their faces hidden from view by balaclavas.

Shit!

Moving back to the middle of the room, Danny swung his head from the window facing the back garden to the window facing the front, trying to decide the best exit.

Front, I need to get to the car.

Swinging the backpack onto his shoulders, Danny held the silenced Sig P365 up and pulled one of the Glock 17s out of its holster. Drawing three big breaths, he tensed and relaxed his muscles. Psyched up, with adrenaline pumping through his veins he gritted his teeth and ran for the front window, firing a single shot from the silenced Sig ahead of him, shattering the tension in the double glazed panels a split second before he twisted and burst out backwards, guns up in a cloud of twinkling glass crystals. Time seemed to stop as he fell, his fingers tapping rapidly on the triggers as he peppered the front of the house and the kill team with bullets before landing arse first into the flowerbed, his back thumping into the backpack.

The soft earth and backpack helped to break his fall, but it was still a painfully hard landing that knocked the wind out of him. He lay there for a moment, arms outstretched, the guns trembling slightly in his grip. After seconds that felt like minutes, no one moved and the air returned to his lungs. He rolled painfully on his side and got on one knee, scanning the road behind him for more assailants before struggling upright. When none presented themselves, he holstered his Glock and shoved the Sig into his trousers before stumbling across to the three bodies in front of his house. Danny rifled through their pockets, pulling out spare gun magazines before picking up their MP5 rifles and heading for his car.

The neighbours' lights were on, and curtains twitched at the sound of gunfire. They disappeared quickly at the sight of bodies and Danny unloading an armoury of weapons into his BMW M4 before climbing in and screaming off down the road.

After zig-zagging through suburbia for a few miles, Danny slowed down to a stop. A light flutter of snow settled on the windscreen as he pulled his phone out of his jeans pocket, the screen lighting up his face as he scrolled through the contacts list. His finger hovered over the number for the Chief of the Secret Intelligence Service, Edward Jenkins. It stayed poised while Danny's mind cycled through the list of people who might want him and his old unit dead. The list for himself was long; the list for the entire team was empty. With a frown across his face, he snapped the phone in half and threw it out the window. He trusted Edward, but didn't trust the people above him, especially the smooth government man known only as Simon. The man had already tried to kill him in Australia over the Command To Kill project. Danny had thought that was all over. Perhaps Simon had decided otherwise and wanted him and anyone who knew him dead after all. It didn't make sense, but then none of this did. Flicking the windscreen wipers on, Danny pulled away from the kerb and drove towards central London and his friends at the, if-the-shit-hits-the-fan meeting point.

4

Danny circled the derelict factory twice, looking for anything out of place before turning into the snow covered car park. He followed a single set of tyre tracks leading to a blue Transit van belonging to his old SAS team member Charles Lemans. He parked next to it, leaving the engine running while he took in the dark, foreboding image of the factory ahead of him. No laser dots on his chest, no automatic fire ripping through the car's thin metal panels; it was safe for now. Turning the engine off, Danny threw the backpack and MP5s over his shoulder and trudged over to the rusty entrance to the factory. The door was slightly ajar, an unlocked padlock hanging on the latch loop attached to the door frame.

Holding the silenced SIG ahead of him, Danny slid silently inside. The empty factory floor was lit by a row of lamps hung from girders on long chains. The place felt like an icebox. Dripping water from holes in the roof

high above echoed as they hit puddles on the cold
concrete floor. A couple of pigeons startled by his
entrance made him spin round. They flew away without
knowing how close they'd been to being blown out of the
sky. A grunting noise coming from the offices at the far
side of the factory floor focused his concentration ahead
of him. Danny moved light-footed across the open
space, pausing by the door before opening it quickly, his
gun locking on the figures ahead of him. Charles Leman
stood facing him, his trousers around his ankles, with
Fergus McKinsey kneeling in front of him.

'Er, do you guys need a minute? I can come back
later,' Danny said with a smirk.

'What can I say, we're a close team,' said Chaz,
looking up with a smile.

Fergus turned to show Chaz's bandaged leg and
blood-soaked rags on the floor.

'Shit, you ok, Chaz?'

'Yeah, stings like a bitch, but the bullet only grazed
the thigh. Some amateur arsehole tried to pop me while
I was taking a shit. I had to stab him in the eye with the
end of the toilet brush while my pants were down.'

'Sounds messy,' Danny chuckled.

'Nah, I managed to nip it off before I stood up,' Chaz
grinned.

'Ok, ok, too much information. What about you Ferg,
you ok?'

'Yeah, Chaz called me straight away. I got Gaynor
and the kids out, sent them to her mother's before Chaz
picked us up. We parked up the street and watched for a

bit, only heading here after a van with a hit team turned up and stormed my house.'

'What about Smudge?'

'I haven't been able to get hold of him. We were going to head over there as soon as you turned up.'

'Right, let's go, you ok to move?' Danny asked Chaz.

'Yeah, good as new,' he replied, pulling his trousers up.

'I see you've had some fun tonight. Nice of you to bring some toys with you,' Fergus said, looking at the silenced Sig and three MP5 submachine guns hung over Danny's shoulder.

'Four of the bastards attacked the house as soon as I got off the phone with you.'

'Who the fuck are these guys and why us?' Fergus said as the three of them headed for the exit.

'I don't know the why, but I do know the who. They work for a drug dealer called Anton. Someone paid him to take us out,' Danny said, checking the coast was clear before heading for the vehicles.

'Do you reckon its revenge for killing Lars Silverman over that sport of Kings business?' said Chaz.

'No, I don't think so. They're all dead, and why now? No, it's been too long,' Danny said, his face serious as he walked to his car.

'Well, who then?'

'Looking at the guns, I'm wondering if the trouble I had in Australia isn't as finished as I thought it was. But I don't see what that has to do with you guys. Let's make sure Smudge is alright first, then we can worry about who's behind this.'

'Roger that,' Fergus said.

'How secure is this place, Chaz?'

'It's safe. No one knows about it. The place has been deserted since my uncle bought it ten years ago. I've only got the keys because I'm pricing it up for demolition. A couple of years from now, this'll be full of million pound flats.'

Danny nodded his approval, and the three of them got in his car with an MP5 sub-machine gun within easy reach by their legs. Danny gave Chaz the silenced Sig and Fergus one of his Glock 17s. Firing up the powerful car, Danny reversed fast, spinning the wheel and dumping it in first as they slid through 180 degrees on the snow, snaking across the car park before straightening up as the tyres found their grip and accelerated the car out the entrance gate.

'So what's this about you and Scott Miller's sister then?' said Fergus, poking his head between them from the back seat.

All eyes looked at Danny.

'Nicki. Er yeah, it's going well. I'm going back to Oz next month to see her. We'll see how it goes from there.'

'Good, I'm pleased for you, mate,' said Chaz.

'Please don't tell me she looks like Scott in a wig,' said Ferg, chuckling from the back seat.

'What's Smudge up to these days?' Danny said, ignoring Fergus's ribbing.

'That means she does then,' mumbled Ferg.

'Him and Diggsy went halves on an old Luton van.

They've been doing removals and house clearances,' said Chaz.

'Diggsy?'

'You remember Diggsy. Terence Diggs. Big black lad, lives on the same estate as Smudge,' said Chaz.

'Oh yeah, dresses like a gangster, shits himself at the first sign of trouble,' said Danny with a smile.

'Jesus, Smudge and Diggsy running a business. What could possibly go wrong?' said Ferg from the back.

The London evening traffic was light, and the drive to Wandsworth passed quickly. Danny pulled up a little way back from Smudge's house, his headlights illuminating a tatty blue Luton van with Smith & Diggs Removals and House Clearance written above a mobile number in uneven sticky letters. Turning the engine off, the three of them sat there, eyes searching the dark in all directions for signs of danger.

'Ok, here we go,' said Danny, clicking the door open.

5

The three exited the car, looking around to check the coast was clear before bringing the MP5s out. Danny moved forward to the van, tucking himself in tight behind the rear corner as he looked down the gun sights at Smudge's front door. Fergus moved up behind him while Chaz walked backwards covering the rear. Moving at a fast walk, Danny headed up the path to Smudge's mid-terrace front door. He reached out to knock, his knuckles freezing just short of the door's shiny surface as he noticed it was slightly ajar. The hairs on the back of his neck stood up. He shot an arm behind him with his hand up to stop Fergus and Chaz coming up the path behind him. Their faces hardened in a heartbeat.

Without a word, they peeled off the path, flattening themselves against the wall on either side of the door. Leaning in, Danny put his ear close to the opening. He could hear muffled voices, low, demanding. A second later a pain filled shriek rang out, followed by Smudge's angry voice telling someone to go fuck themselves. It came from somewhere on the far side of the house. Placing his hand on the door, Danny pushed it open millimetre at a time, testing the hinges for creaks. He opened it silently, just far enough to peek inside. The hallway was dark, its interior only visible from a sliver of light from the kitchen at the far end.

'Talk. Where's Pearson, Leman and McKinsey?' came an Eastern European accented voice from the kitchen.

'Piss off, you nonces,' growled Smudge in response.

'Fucking bag him,' came the voice again.

Pushing the door a little further, Danny slid inside, beckoning Fergus and Chaz to follow him. All three moved silently down the hall, MP5s up, muscles tensed, the adrenaline building in anticipation of action. Stopping just short of the wedge of light from the kitchen, Danny leant forward just enough to see through the gap. Diggsy lay on the floor semi-conscious, one of his eyes swollen shut and blood running from his nose. Smudge sat tied to a chair, gritting his teeth angrily as he strained against his bonds. A guy wearing a balaclava pulled a plastic carrier bag over his head, twisting it tight around his neck. The plastic across Smudge's open mouth alternated between puffing out and sucked in as Smudge desperately tried to draw breath. At the same time, two other men dressed in black bomber jackets, jeans and trainers stood in front of Smudge, taking it in turns to punch him in the stomach. Spotting the attacker's guns sitting on the kitchen table, Danny pushed the door slowly open. He, Chaz and Fergus moved quietly into the kitchen until they stood side by side along the far wall.

'So, who do you reckon these bunch of wankers are?' Fergus said loudly to draw their attention.

'I don't know, but I think that's our man, Smudge, with a carrier bag over his head,' said Chaz.

'Oh no, Chaz, that's not just any carrier bag, that's an M&S carrier bag,' said Danny, his eyes staring dark and dangerous at the three men looking confused in front of them.

The bag swung in their direction as Smudge turned his head at the sound of their voices.

'Oh, so sorry, guys, I stand corrected. Who are these bunch of posh wankers?' said Fergus, watching the three men as they looked from him to their guns on the table and back to him again.

'Don't do it, don't you fucking move,' Chaz growled.

'Fucking do the bastards,' came Smudge's muffled cry, the carrier bag swinging from left to right as he spoke.

Smudge's outburst panicked the men into going for their guns on the table. Danny, Fergus and Chaz cut them down with a quick burst of fire before they got their guns a millimetre off the table, the impact of the bullets sending the three men flying backwards into a heap by the back door. The room fell into silence. Nobody moved until the gun smoke drifted away.

'That was a bit tense. You got any beers, Smudge?' Chaz finally said, heading for the fridge.

'Do you mind taking this fucking bag off my head first?' Smudge replied, swinging his head in the plastic bag towards Chaz's voice.

Chaz whipped the bag off as he passed, while Fergus pulled a knife from the block on the kitchen worktop and sliced the gaffer tape holding Smudge to the chair.

'Cheers, Ferg. Here, give us a hand with Diggsy.'

The two of them picked Diggsy up and sat him in a chair, splashing his face with water until he came round.

'You alright, Smudge?' said Danny as Chaz chucked a beer can across the kitchen to him.

'Yeah, I'm ok, they punch like a bunch of girls. Thanks for coming to get me. Any idea who these wankers are?'

'No, but someone's gone to a lot of trouble trying to eliminate all of us, so let's drink up, send Diggsy home, and get the hell out of here before more of them arrive,' Danny said, putting the beer can in Smudge's hand and patting him on the shoulder.

'You found anything, Chaz?' said Ferg.

'Er, not much, no wallets, no ID, just cash and burner phones.'

'Just bag it all with the guns and let's get out of here. We'll make camp at the old factory and figure out what the hell's going on,' Danny said, grabbing a roll of bin bags from under the sink and throwing them to Fergus.

A couple of minutes later, they checked the coast was clear and headed for the car, sending a dazed and confused Diggsy home before getting in.

'Poor sod, he'll have nightmares about this for weeks,'

said Smudge as Danny drove away, criss-crossing through the suburban streets until he was sure they weren't followed, heading back towards the factory when he was satisfied.

'So what do you reckon, Staff?' Ferg said, naturally reverting to their SAS days when Danny was in charge as Staff Sergeant.

'I don't know. I'm going to drop you lot off and put some feelers out.'

'You sure you don't want us to come?' said Chaz.

'Nah, I'll be ok. Remember, guys, no messages, no phones, we keep off grid until we figure out what we're dealing with,' Danny said, turning into the factory car park, glad to see the fresh snow had covered the tracks made when they'd left, with no fresh tracks to indicate a waiting danger.

6

Paul Greenwood sat in his home office working on staff schedules for a large upcoming Greenwood Security event. His wife came in and put a mug of coffee on the desk.

'I'm off to bed,' she said, putting her arms around his neck as she leant round and kissed him on the cheek.

'Ok love,' he said, still engrossed in the spreadsheets.

'Don't work too late,' she said, leaving him to it.

'I won't,' he called after her.

He worked on for about twenty minutes, pausing when he remembered the coffee on his desk. It had cooled to lukewarm, but he gulped it down anyway. A draught caught his neck as someone entered the room behind him.

'I thought you'd gone to bed.'

'Not much chance of that tonight,' came a familiar voice.

Paul spun the chair around to find Danny sitting on

the small Chesterfield sofa by the door, the two Glock 17s poking out from under his open jacket.

'Shoot me if you like, you're still not getting a pay rise,' Paul said with a wry smile.

'Mmm, the thought did cross my mind,' Danny said, his face softening before breaking into a smile.

'I take it from your current attire there's a problem.'

'Good to see all those years in British Intelligence weren't wasted, mate. Yes, there's a big fucking problem. I've got four dead Eastern Europeans at my house, and another four at Smudge's and Chaz's.'

'Are you all ok?' Paul said, concern written on his face.

'Yeah, Chaz got clipped with a flesh wound, but we're all ok.'

'Do you know who sent them?'

'All I've got is a drug dealer called Anton,' said Danny, rubbing his eyes, tiredness setting in after the adrenaline build up from the earlier action had disappeared.

'What do you need?' Paul said without a second thought.

'Talk to Edward, in person, not on the phone. I don't know how far this goes. See what he can find out.'

'Ok, anything else? Do you need somewhere to stay?' Paul said, noticing how tired his friend looked.

'No, I've got somewhere. There's something else. I need to find Simon,' Danny said, his face turning deadly serious.

'Do you think that's a good idea?'

'It doesn't make sense that he'd target my old unit, or use a drug dealer to do it, but I've gotta know this isn't some twisted revenge for that Command To Kill business in Australia.'

'Ok, I'll see what I can find out. How do I get hold of you?' Paul said, getting up and checking the hall to make sure his wife hadn't woken up.

'My office, the third drawer down in my desk, you'll find a new pay as you go phone, turn it on at 10 a.m. tomorrow. I'll call you.'

'Ok. By the way, who was that woman earlier, the one you were looking decidedly unhappy about talking to? The one waiting for you in reception on your way out of the office tonight?'

'The woman?' Danny said, the excitement of the night putting her out of his mind. 'The woman!' he repeated, searching his jeans pockets until he fished her card out.

'And?'

'She's a journalist looking into a target we were after back in Afghanistan, an arms dealer nicknamed the Wolf. He killed her father when he got too close to discovering his identity. She's found his notebook and camera with details and pictures of my unit from the day he died.'

'Don't you think that's a bit of a coincidence?' Paul said, turning back to his computer screen after a series of emails pinging into his inbox caught his eye. 'Do you need money?'

He turned back when he got no answer to see an

empty room. Sticking his head into the hall, he looked around in the silence at an empty house.

***

Heading through the streets of London towards the factory, Danny turned over Amanda Wallace's business card in his hand. He pulled over and took the pay as you go phone out of his pocket. It took a moment to power up and get signal before he could dial the number on the card. When it connected, the call clicked straight over to answerphone.

'Hi, Miss Wallace, this is Daniel Pearson. You came to my office earlier today. We need to talk. I have reason to believe you may be in danger. Don't go home, check yourself into a hotel and talk to no one. I'll call again tomorrow afternoon.'

When he'd finished, he powered the phone back off, took the battery and sim card out and pocketed them before pulling away and continuing his journey.

7

'Mr Hake,' Arthur Montgomery answered, his voice matter of fact as he got in the back of his chauffeur driven Bentley.

'Anton has disposed of the bodies. I've had a clean-up crew take care of any evidence and I'm just waiting for the glazer to put a new bedroom window in at Pearson's house. We should be out of here in ten minutes,' said MI5 agent, Barry Hake. He didn't address Arthur by name. He didn't know it or want to know it. The voice on the end of the phone made the money happen. That's all he cared about. He'd been recruited by a drug dealer, Anton Kasovich, when his wife divorced him over his runaway gambling habits and he needed money desperately. At first, it had been a little information here, a little there. Then, when they knew his greed for money outweighed his morals, they passed him up the chain to do more important work for Arthur and Vincent.

'And the police? I hear a neighbour called them,'

Arthur said quietly before muting the phone to address his driver. 'The Lansdowne Club please, Roger.'

'Yes sir.'

'Go on, Mr Hake.'

'I informed the Chief of Police of an MI5 active operation in the area. He's to keep his officers out during its execution. We visited the neighbours and made them sign a gagging order, matters of national security with the threat of a fifteen year jail term if they breach it. It put the fear of god up them; they won't talk.'

'Good, now find those men and the woman and eliminate them. The clock is ticking, Mr Hake.'

'Ok, but this has gone way outside of our agreement. We were supposed to clean up Pearson and his men, not this bloodbath. If Utting and I are found out at SIS, they'll throw the book at us. We want more money,' said Hake, the nervousness in his voice becoming more apparent as he finished with his demand.

There was a tense pause as Arthur contemplated his response. 'I will talk to the client. In the meantime, find them and be quick about it.'

Arthur hung up before Hake could answer. He took a moment to collect his thoughts, then dialled another number.

'Is it done?'

'Unfortunately not. Pearson and his men got away.'

'Got away? What do you mean, got away?' the client's voice was clearly irritated.

'They killed them all and disappeared. I did say using

Anton's men was a mistake, they were no match for SAS trained soldiers. I've got Hake and Utting using all of SIS's resources to locate them,' said Arthur, his voice still calm and steady.

'Christ, bloody Anton Kasovich, my instructions were to do this discreetly. A trail of dead men in the capital is not what I call discreet. Wait until the media gets a hold on this. There'll be a massive shitstorm. I can't afford this kind of publicity before the eighteenth.'

'And you won't have to. The situation has been contained. Anton removed the bodies and Hake had a clean-up crew remove any evidence.'

'Good, let's hope Hake and Utting find them quickly.'

'About that, they want more money.'

'Mmm, ok, pay them. What about that damn journalist woman, the one who started all this?'

'We lost her and her phone's gone down so we can't track her. I've got Peeler involved. He's got men out covering her apartment and Hake's trying to pull her phone records to find out who she's been in contact with. We'll find her.'

'This is a disaster. Get on top of this, Arthur, whatever it takes. If I go down, so do you,' he said angrily.

'It's all under control, Vincent, you concentrate on the eighteenth, I'll concentrate on getting rid of our little problem,' Arthur replied before ending the call, his voice still calm as his mind ticked logically through all angles of the problem at hand.

'We're here, sir,' Roger said, exiting the car to move swiftly around the back to open the passenger door.

Arthur looked up to see the subtle sign above a black shiny door that indicated the Lansdowne private members club. A club where the rich, the powerful, and the elite mixed and made decisions that moulded the country.

'Thank you, Roger. Why don't you pop off and get something to eat? I shall be a couple of hours.'

'Yes sir,' Roger said, shutting the door behind him before scooting back around to the driver's side.

Arthur climbed the steps, the shiny black door opening before he had to knock. An immaculately dressed man stood to one side to gesture him in.

'Thank you, Leonard. Is the Prime Minister here already?'

'Yes, Mr Montgomery, he's at your usual table.'

'Excellent,' Arthur said, heading through the lounge to the dining room.

'Can I get you anything, sir?' Leonard said, following closely behind.

'Er, yes, I'll have a Scotch on the rocks, the good stuff, eighteen year old Glen Moray please.'

'Certainly, sir,' Leonard said, disappearing off to fulfil the order.

'Evening John. I hope you haven't been waiting long,' Arthur said, shaking the Prime Minister's hand before sitting.

'No, no, my dear fellow, I've only just arrived.'

'Excellent, and you have a drink already, even better,' Arthur said, nodding to Leonard as he placed his Scotch on the table along with a couple of menus.

'Vincent not joining us tonight, Arthur?' the PM asked.

'No, I'm afraid he's otherwise engaged, something to do with his humanitarian aid charity, a gala dinner I think.'

'Well, that is why he's Vincent Benedict MBE after all, and one of the reasons he's going to be announced as the Foreign Secretary in the cabinet reshuffle on the eighteenth,' the PM said, leaning in and speaking softly.

'Yes, and he's very much looking forward to it, John.'

'You know there is a place for you, if you want it,' the PM said with a nod and a smile.

'That's very kind of you, John, but I prefer to stay behind the lines. I'm far more suited to being a special advisor to the government. It allows me the freedom and anonymity to best serve my clients' needs.'

'Absolutely your choice, but if you ever change your mind, the offer still stands.'

8

'Aw, damn, my phone's out of battery,' Amanda said, dumping it back in her bag.

'Do you need to borrow mine?'

'No, it's ok. Thanks, Diane, I needed this. It's been a pretty shitty day, and a night out is just what I needed,' said Amanda, clinking her glass against her friends as they sat in the booth of a Soho wine bar.

'That's ok, Barry's away all week so you're welcome to crash at mine tonight. So tell me, what happened when you went to see the action man?' Diane said, ignoring a group of young men grinning and laughing as they tried to make eye contact with her and Amanda.

'It didn't go well. As soon as I mentioned the SAS, he got, well, he got very rude, and a little bit scary. Pretty much threw me out,' Amanda said, smiling at one of the lads at the bar.

'Stop it, don't encourage them,' said Diane.

'Ok, ok, I'm just having a bit of fun. Oh god, he's

coming over,' Amanda said before the two of them burst out laughing.

'Evening, ladies. Can I get you a drink?'

'Thank you very much. I'll have a large white wine and the same for my friend,' she said, giving him an encouraging look.

They burst out laughing again as he disappeared to the bar.

'You're terrible. Anyway, what about that posh bloke, Gilbert's mate, the political advisor?'

'I don't even know his name. Gilbert, being Gilbert, just got him on the phone and made me tell the guy the whole story about my father and the Wolf, the pictures and the notebook. To be honest, he gave me the creeps. He was so adamant that I give the photos and notebook to Gilbert so he could look into it for me. They're all I have left of my father and I didn't feel like handing them over to some creepy old guy I don't even know.'

'So what are you going to do?'

'Well, right now I'm going to get drunk and have some fun with our new friends,' Amanda said as the man walked back with the drinks and his friends in tow.

9

Having driven around the block twice to make sure he wasn't followed, Danny turned through the gates to the old factory. A dusting of fresh snow had fallen since he'd left, letting him see his earlier ins and outs, but didn't show any fresh tracks made in the last half hour or so. He drove down next to Chaz's van, got out and headed for the entrance. Pausing at the door, he turned towards a pile of rubble and metal sheeting.

'Is that your teeth chattering or your bollocks rattling, Ferg?'

'It's fucking both, mate. Tell Smudge to come and take watch before I turn into a popsicle,' came Ferg's voice, followed by an MP5 sub-machine gun and his grinning face popping out from under a metal sheet.

'Alright, mate, I'll send him out in a minute,' Danny said, grinning back before heading inside.

He moved across the empty factory floor and entered the offices, surprised to be greeted by a wall of warm air as he entered. Smudge and Chaz had plugged in a row of new fan heaters along the far wall, their packaging and boxes piled up in the corner. The floor was littered with blow-up beds, duvets, and pillows.

'Tesco Extra, mate, hope you don't mind, but we borrowed some cash out of your bag for provisions,' said Smudge, sitting next to Chaz at a table with a brand new microwave, a kettle, and an assortment of microwave meals, tea, coffee and milk.

'No, that's fine. Fix us a brew, Smudge, then relieve Ferg before he gets frostbite. I'll take the next watch.'

'Ok boss,' Smudge said, clicking the kettle on.

'So, did you find anything out?' said Chaz.

'I've got Paul looking into it. Hopefully, we'll have more answers tomorrow.'

'We'll just have to bed in and make ourselves comfortable. Curry or lasagne?' Chaz said, holding up two ready meals.

'Stick the curry in mate, it might warm me up. Cheers Smudge,' Danny said as Smudge put a coffee in front of him and headed off to relieve Fergus.

'Roger that,' Chaz said, punching the buttons on the microwave.

'There's something else,' Danny said, pulling Amanda Wallace's business card from his pocket.

'Oh yeah, do tell,' Chaz replied, his interest piqued.

'Do you remember when the top brass got their knickers in a twist over an arms dealer called the Wolf?'

'I remember half a dozen hairy bollocks missions into Takhar Province trying to find the slippery bastard trading arms for heroin worth millions more than the guns on the open market.'

'That's him. The Taliban had so much of the bloody stuff they didn't know what to do with it. Anyway, you remember the last mission to that shitty one goat village with a makeshift airstrip at the foot of the mountains?'

'Yeah, we missed the guy by seconds. His plane was just taking off as we arrived. Never heard of him again,' said Chaz, a puzzled look on his face as to where this was going.

'Right, bear with me. Remember that crazy fucking pain in the arse journalist, always turning up trying to get a scoop on the Wolf? We confiscated his cameras and deleted the pictures a few times when we caught him snapping us. The Wolf spotted him in a hut by the airfield as he was getting ready to leave, let rip on him with an AK47.'

'Yeah, we got him on a chopper back to camp. He died on the way to the hospital. What's this got to do with anything?'

'The guy's name was David Wallace. Yesterday his daughter, Amanda Wallace, turns up at my work asking about her father. Apparently she's been going through his stuff and found a notebook he had while investigating the Wolf. She also had his camera containing photos of our unit and a picture of the Wolf, presumably just before he shot him,' Danny said, taking a drink of his coffee.

'And what did you do?' Chaz said, sitting forward with interest.

'I told her I couldn't talk about anything we did in the regiment and to destroy the photos of us. It was years ago. I didn't think anything of it, and who the hell cares about the Wolf now anyway? Everyone has pulled out of the country?'

'Yeah, I see what you're saying. It's a bit of a coincidence though. She turns up and everyone starts trying to kill us.'

'I know. I left a message on her phone. I'm going to try to talk to her tomorrow.'

'Get the kettle on. It's brass fucking monkey weather out there,' said Fergus, bursting in before hugging a heater. 'What? You look like I just interrupted you shagging,' he continued, looking at Danny and Chaz falling into silence.

'Shut up, you big idiot,' Danny said, chuckling before clicking the kettle on.

'It's alright, you two, carry on, there's no judgement here,' Fergus said with a wide grin on his face.

10

Entering the SIS building and headquarters of MI6 and MI5 located on the banks of the River Thames, Chief of the Secret Intelligence Service Edward Jenkins passed through security, the staff greeting him as he headed for the lift. His face was serious as he turned over what his friend Paul Greenwood had told him at their breakfast meeting. The doors opened, and he exited, swiping his pass card to enter the SIS offices.

'My office please, James,' he said as he passed a senior Intelligence Officer.

'Yes sir,' James replied, getting up from his chair and following Edward.

Leaning back in his chair, Barry Hake stuck his head out of his cubicle and watched James follow Edward into his office.

'James, what information do we have on last night's shootings in Walthamstow, Wandsworth and Harrow?' Edward asked, turning on his computer and logging onto the Secret Intelligence Service database.

'Sir?' James said, puzzled.

'Eight bodies armed with automatic weapons, links to a drug dealer called Anton.'

'Sorry sir, we've had no reports of any shootings last night.'

Edward looked from James to his computer screen. After scrolling through the reports, he frowned.

'Ok, that will be all, James,' he said, dismissing him.

As soon as James left the office, Edward picked up his phone. 'Kathleen, can you get Police Chief Ryan McGillan on the phone for me please?' he said, replacing the receiver and looking out the window at the Thames, deep in thought. The phone buzzed a couple of minutes later.

'Yes.'

'Chief McGillan for you, sir.'

'Thank you, Kathleen,' Edward said, waiting for the click before talking further. 'Chief McGillan.'

'Mr Jenkins, how can I help you?'

'I wanted to know whether you had any reports of shootings last night, automatic weapons, eight dead in Walthamstow, Wandsworth, and Harrow?'

'I'm sorry, I don't understand. I had a notification of an active MI5 operation in those areas with the order not to intervene,' said the Chief, puzzled.

'An order? On whose authority?'

'Well, on yours, I've got the QC23 order you emailed in front of me.'

Edward turned to his computer and moved the mouse

to his secure mail server. Opening it, he sat back frowning when he saw the email to the Chief in his sent folder.

'Ok, thank you, Chief,' he said, replacing the phone receiver.

He sat there for a minute before standing and looking out over his office at all the agents, trying to figure out who'd sent the email from his office.

***

Sitting in his cubicle, Barry Hake had received Amanda Wallace's phone records from her provider, and was putting a list of names and addresses to the incoming and outgoing calls. When he'd finished, he printed them out and tucked them in his pocket before wandering across to Peter Utting's cubicle. He gave him a tap on the shoulder and the two of them slid out of the office. They took the lift down to the underground car park and drove out into the London traffic, Utting driving while Hake made a call.

'I have a list of addresses from Amanda Wallace's phone records. We're going to check them out now.'

11

After a night of broken sleep and turns keeping watch, they assumed they were safe at the factory for now. Danny ate microwave lasagne for breakfast, washed down with gallons of coffee until the caffeine pushed away the tiredness. He stripped and checked all the weapons, splitting them up between the four of them. At five to ten, he turned on his mobile and waited for Paul's call, which happened predictably dead on ten.

'Paul.'

'Morning, Danny, everyone ok?'

'Yeah, if whoever's after us knew we were here, I guess they would've been here by now. What do you know?' Danny said, pleased to hear his friend's voice.

'I spoke to Edward this morning. He's just got back to me. Whoever did this is well connected. The bodies disappeared and someone from MI5 faked an order from Edward to keep the police from investigating.'

'Simon, it's got to be Simon. Did you find out where

he is?' said Danny, getting angry at the thought.

'Yes, but don't go charging in like a bull in a china shop. If you're wrong, he could be the one who could help you,' Paul said, trying to calm Danny down.

'Where is he, Paul?'

'He's in a meeting at the Home Office building at the moment, then he has a suit fitting at Davies and Son on Savile Row at eleven. Danny, don't do anything stupid.'

'Thanks, Paul, this phone will be off now. I'll be in touch soon.'

'Ok, be careful.'

'I always am,' Danny said, hanging up before pulling the sim and battery out of the phone and chucking it into the rubbish pile in the corner.

He took a new pay as you go phone out of his bag and looked at his watch.

I'll call Amanda Wallace after I talk to Simon.

'Right, boys, we've gotta move. Anyone need a new suit?' Danny said to puzzled faces.

***

Simon walked briskly out of the Home Office building to his waiting car parked on double yellow lines outside. His driver was already out and holding the door open for him.

'Thank you, Michael, take me to Davies and Son please.'

'Yes sir.'

He sat back and relaxed, browsing through a few files from the multitude of folders in his briefcase as the car drove smoothly through the thirty-minute journey to Savile Row. His driver pulled in behind a blue Transit van parked in the loading bay outside the immaculately presented Davies and Son tailors.

'I'll be about an hour, Michael,' Simon said, getting out the door before Michael had a chance to get out and open it for him.

'Very good, sir.' Michael said. He wasn't worried about traffic wardens. His National Security Council ID card was enough to send them scurrying off to the next traffic offender.

'Good afternoon, sir. Would you follow me into the fitting room?' his tailor said nervously, his hand shaking as he gestured toward the back room.

'Good afternoon, Giles. Is everything alright?' Simon asked, following him through the shop.

As soon as he'd entered the fitting room, Fergus appeared from behind a clothes rail full of suits and marched Giles away to the stockroom at gunpoint. Simon turned at the sound of movement to see Smudge locking the shop door, and Chaz drawing the curtain that separated the fitting room from the front of the shop. Simon looked around the empty fitting room. If he was nervous, it didn't show. At the far end of the room, the cubicle curtain slid slowly back to reveal Danny, his face set in stone and eyes staring directly into Simon's, dark and menacing, his right arm locked as he pointed the silenced Sig at Simon's head.

'Well, well, well, Mr Pearson. Despite your obvious need for a good suit, I'm guessing that's not why you're here. Do tell, old boy, I have a very busy schedule today,' Simon said, calm and collected.

'Are you trying to kill me and my unit?'

There was a slight pause and the faintest flicker of confusion on Simon's face before he covered it and answered. 'Mmm, as attractive as that thought would be, at this precise moment in time, no, I am not trying to kill you or your little bunch of friends.'

'And it's not your Pentagon friend, Joel Stilwell, in retaliation for Australia?' Danny growled, the gun still held steady as a rock, his eyes never leaving Simon's.

'Dear boy, Joel Stilwell is looking after the security of the United States. He and I, for that matter, have far more important things to do than run around sanctioning petty revenge killings. Believe it or not, I quite admire you for what you did in Australia.'

This time, it was Danny's turn to pause. Whichever way he turned it over in his head, he knew Simon was telling the truth. Without a word, Danny circled Simon before lowering the gun and disappearing through the curtain.

'Don't be a stranger, Mr Pearson. I could still use a man like you,' Simon called after him.

'No, you couldn't,' came Danny's growled reply, followed by the faint sound of the shop door closing.

Simon smiled as he casually slid his suit jacket off and placed it on a hanger on the clothes rail. He pulled a wad of notes out of his trouser pocket held together by a silver money clip and pulled a few free as a shaky Giles entered the fitting room.

'For your discretion,' he said, handing the notes to him.

'Thank you, sir,' Giles replied, before pulling his measuring tape from around his neck.

12

Amanda dragged herself out of bed and stood up. Her head spun a couple of times before thumping in protest. She groaned when she saw 11:20 on her watch. Grabbing her bag from the chair, she opened it and rummaged around for her phone, cursing when she pressed the power on button and nothing happened. The recollection of a flat phone battery taking a little time to register through the hangover.

'Diane, have you got a phone charger I can borrow?' she said, padding down the hall into the kitchen of her friend's flat.

'Er, yeah, hang on,' said Diane, hugging a coffee at the kitchen table, her eyes bloodshot and hair sticking up all over the place.

'You alright?' Amanda said with a chuckle.

'This is your fault, encouraging those boys. Here you go,' Diane groaned, pulling a charger from the kitchen drawer crammed with everything that might come in handy one day.

'Free drinks all night though. Thanks,' she said, taking the charger and plugging it in, frowning at the red battery symbol with the charging lightning bolt flashing on the screen.

'Yeah, did you see their faces when we went home?'

'That's their fault, horny little bastards. I didn't ask them to buy us drinks. Alright if I take a shower?' she said, sniffing her armpit and pulling a face.

'Yeah, go ahead,' Diane said with a laugh.

***

Arthur Montgomery sat in the kitchen of his six-bedroom townhouse in the affluent St John's Wood area of London. He sipped his tea and read the newspaper, folding it carefully and placing it neatly to one side when his phone rang.

'Mr Hake.'

'Amanda Wallace's phone just came on.'

'You've got a location?'

'She's in a block of flats in Paddington, 25 Dorchester Place.'

'Can you be more specific?'

'No, the building's twenty-two storeys high. Best I can do is tell you it's a flat facing the front of the building. We're going through the phone records to see if we can find a match for a resident in the building.'

'Thank you, Hake. Call me if you get a match. I'll get Mr Peeler to investigate.'

Arthur hung up and flicked through his contacts

before pressing the call button.

'Mr Peeler, the young lady we discussed, is in a residential tower block at 25 Dorchester Place, Paddington. Hake is trying to narrow that location to a flat. I'll call you when I have more information.'

'Yes sir, we're on our way.'

***

Showered and dressed, Amanda returned to the kitchen. Diane was dressed and looking more together.

'Right, I've got to go to work now. Just close the door on the latch when you leave,' Diane said, moving in and giving her friend a hug.

'Ok. Thanks, Diane.'

'Oh, your phone's been buzzing away. Somebody's popular. Call me, yeah,' she said, heading out the door.

'Yeah, will do, bye.'

Amanda walked up to the phone and picked it up. One voice message and three missed calls, number withheld. She pressed the button for the voice message.

"Hi, Miss Wallace, this is Daniel Pearson. You came to my office earlier today. We need to talk. I have reason to believe you may be in danger. Don't go home, check yourself into a hotel and talk to no one. I will call again tomorrow afternoon."

Danny's voice froze her to the spot. She had to play it back three times before it sank in. She was standing there stunned when the phone rang again with the same withheld number message displaying on the screen.

'Er, hello,' she said quietly.

'Miss Wallace, it's Daniel Pearson. Did you get my message?' Danny said with urgency in his voice.

'Yes, what's this about? What danger?'

'After talking to you yesterday, somebody tried to have me and my unit killed. I think it has something to do with your father's investigation. Have you spoken to anyone else about this?'

'I tried to talk to the MoD to find out who you were, but they wouldn't talk to me. I eventually recognised you from an old newspaper report of you and your friend Scott Miller, something to do with a cyber attack on the banking systems. Oh, and I spoke to some government advisor on the phone. He was a friend of a friend, but I didn't take him up on his offer of help.'

Danny grabbed a scrap of cardboard and a pen. 'Where are you? We'll come to you.'

'I'm at a friend's, flat 38, 25 Dorchester Place, Paddington,' she said, a hint of fear showing in her voice.

'Ok, we're on our way. Turn your phone off and put it inside the microwave. They won't be able to track it in there. Have you got that?' Danny said forcefully to make her focus.

'Er yes, in the microwave, got it.'

'Alright, sit tight. We'll be there soon.'

13

As Amanda turned off her phone and placed it in the microwave of her friend's fifth-floor flat, two black Land Rover Discoverys pulled up in the slush outside the main entrance to the tower block. Two men got out of the vehicle in front and approached the one behind as its window lowered.

'You two stay here and cover the front. If she comes out, grab her. We don't kill her until we have the notebook and photos, ok? Me and Billings will go to the top and work our way down. Call us on the radio if you see anything,' he said, heading for the entrance after the driver nodded.

He pressed the button for a top floor flat and waited for a response.

'Hello,' came a metallic answer.

'This is Detective Inspector Grant Peeler, sir. Would you mind buzzing us in please?' Peeler said, holding his warrant card up to the door camera.

After a pause, the lock buzzed open, and the two men stepped inside. They entered the lift, trying to ignore the smell of piss as they pressed the button for the top floor.

'Jesus, what a shit hole,' Billings said, screwing his face up.

'Come on, let's get this done,' said Peeler, stepping out onto the top floor.

He headed for the nearest flat and hammered on the door. 'Police, can you open the door please?'

It opened just wide enough to see a worried face peer around it.

'Detective Inspector Grant Peeler, madam, do you know or have you seen this woman?' he said, shoving his badge in her face with one hand before shoving a picture of Amanda Wallace in her face with the other.

'Er, no, Officer I—'

Billings cut her dead by barging past her. 'Mind if we come in and check? Thank you very much, madam,' he said, not giving her a chance to answer.

He did a quick circuit of the flat before walking out.

'Thank you very much,' Peeler said, pulling the door shut on the confused woman before walking across to Billings, banging on the door of the next flat.

***

'That's it, pull up over there, Chaz,' Danny said a little way back from the tower block.

The three of them sat in the front of the van while Smudge leant in to look between them from the back, scanning the road ahead for signs of trouble.

'What do you think?' said Fergus.

'I don't like the look of the Land Rovers,' Chaz said, squinting to see if anyone was in them.

'Yeah, this isn't the kind of estate where the owners can afford sixty-grand motors, unless they're drug dealers,' said Danny, getting a glimpse of the passenger in the nearside wing mirror.

'Nah, they're a bit grandad for dealers. Your BMW M4's more their choice,' said Smudge from the back.

'Thanks for that little nugget of information, Smudge,' Danny said, giving him a look.

'What? Just saying.'

'Front's a no go, there's got to be another way in,' said Fergus.

'There must be a fire exit around the back. Fire regs would demand it, wouldn't they?' said Chaz, looking at the others.

'I reckon so. Drive past them and swing it around back, Chaz. Let's have a look,' Danny said.

Chaz drove on. Danny had his arm up and head against the passenger window, obscuring the view of him from the two men in the Land Rover and making it look like he was asleep. He looked back at the occupants in the van's wing mirror as they passed, noting two white guys, their heads turned towards the entrance, taking no notice of the van that had just driven past. Moving around the back of the building, Chaz parked by the bins with a direct line of sight of a fire door to the rear of a small stairwell.

'Wait here and keep the engine running, Chaz. If the

shit hits the fan, call us on the burner phone, ok?'

'Roger that, boss.'

The three of them got out, Fergus and Smudge concealing as much of their MP5 submachine guns under their jackets as they could. Danny pulled the silenced SIG and pulled the trigger at the glass in the fire exit door. A couple of metallic pings emanated from the barrel as the bullets punched through the glass. Sliding the gun into his shoulder holster, Danny followed the bullets up with a punch through the shattering glass to push the release bar down so he could pull the door open.

They entered the small stairwell. Danny walked forward and looked through the glass of an internal fire door opposite. It gave him a view right through the building to the lifts, main stairwell, and front entrance. Beyond that, he could see the road and the two men keeping watch in one of the Land Rovers. Without turning away from the glass, Danny waved Fergus and Smudge up the stairs. He backed away and followed once they'd reached the first-floor landing. Fergus looked along the submachine gun sights up the centre of the stairwell, while Smudge covered down the stairs as Danny came up. They repeated this process, rapidly working up the floors until they reached the fifth. Taking the lead, Danny darted his head through the fire door to the landing. With no one in sight, he tucked the gun away and turned back to Fergus and Smudge.

'Hide those. The last thing we need is someone calling the police. We'd have an armed response unit on our arse in no time.'

Weapons tucked under their coats, the three of them walked as casually as they could to flat 38.

'Miss Wallace, it's Daniel Pearson,' Danny said, knocking lightly on the door.

A few seconds later, he heard the rattle of the chain coming off the door before it opened far enough to see Amanda's frightened face.

Danny gave the best reassuring smile he could. She opened the door further, her hand going to her mouth when she glimpsed the Sig on one side and Glock on the other through his open jacket.

'It's ok, I'm not here to hurt you, ok?' Danny said, stepping into the flat, followed by Smudge and Fergus.

14

A Volvo turned towards Dorchester Place. Hake pulled up behind the Land Rover and got out with Utting. Hake tapped on the Land Rover's window, which immediately slid down.

'Where's Peeler?'

'He's up top with Billings. They're working their way down the building.'

'Call him. She's at a friend's flat, fifth floor, flat 38.'

The other guy in the Land Rover relayed the information over the radio.

Peeler's voice came back a second later. 'You come up. We're on our way down to the fifth now.'

The two men got out of the Land Rover, sliding their coats off to reveal tactical vests with Police written on the back and front. They pulled out police-issued Glock 17s while Hake and Utting followed them toward the entrance, pulling their own handguns as they went.

'Police, hold that door,' the officer in the lead shouted

as a woman pushing a pram came out.

'You two take the lift,' he said to Hake and Utting, as he moved into the foyer with his partner.

The two men split as they passed the lift doors, one heading up the main staircase while the other pushed the fire door open to the rear stairs.

'Proper fucking Rambos, them two,' Utting joked, pressing the button for the lift, his face dropping as the doors opened and the smell of stale piss hit his nostrils.

***

'Danny, time to go, boss,' Smudge said, pulling the MP5 out from under his coat as he looked out the living room window at four armed men heading for the entrance to the tower block.

'What the hell's going on?' Amanda said, anger, confusion and frustration hitting her all at once.

'Have you got the notebook and photos?' Danny said, his voice commanding as he looked at her with an unwavering stare.

'Yes, here,' she said, holding her bag up.

'Good, we need to leave now. There are men on their way up here to kill you because of something in there,' Danny said, taking her by the arm and following Fergus as he took the lead.

The coast was clear as they exited the flat and headed back towards the rear stairwell. The sound of the lift pinging, followed by the doors opening beside them kicked Smudge into action. He turned to face a surprised Hake and Utting. Moving on instinct, Smudge cracked Utting hard on the nose with the butt of the MP5 as both men panicked to pull their guns from beneath their coats. Flipping the submachine gun around, Smudge pointed it at Hake just as he freed his gun, freezing him to the spot. Utting stood next to him, holding his nose to stem the bleeding as he struggled to see through watery eyes. No one moved as the lift dinged and the doors slid shut, the sound of Hake's swearing fading away as the lift descended. Ahead of them, Fergus poked his head over the balcony of the main stairwell, only to see the Police lettering on the guy from the Land Rover's vest and the barrel of his gun looking back up at him. Pulling his head back, Fergus got out of sight just in time to miss the gun fire from below. Bullets whizzed past, taking chips out of the concrete ceiling above his head before ricocheting into the wall behind him.

'Go,' Fergus shouted, giving a short burst of fire over the bannister as Danny pulled Amanda through the fire door to the rear stairs, with Smudge following close behind. Footsteps running down the stairs somewhere above them, making Danny chance a look. His eyes locked on Peeler's, three floors above. Danny tucked back in as Billings pointed his gun, leaving him aiming at empty space. Heading down as fast as they could, the group got halfway between the second and third floors when Danny put his hand up, stopping the party dead in its tracks. In the instant silence, he could hear footsteps on the stairs directly underneath them. Holstering his gun, Danny gripped the bannister with both hands and jumped out into the void in the centre of the stairs. He put his booted feet together as he swung himself into the stairs directly below them, planting two feet squarely into the chest of the police officer coming up from below. The blow slammed the man into the wall, forcing the air out of him as he dropped his gun and crumpled to the floor. Shaking off a painful landing on the hard steps, Danny rolled himself upright as the others ran down the stairs to join him. Smudge kicking the officer in the bollocks as he passed just for good measure.

'Keep them in their box,' Danny ordered, stopping just short of the ground floor. Smudge darted a look up the centre of the stairwell, letting rip with several blasts of semi-automatic fire. Peeler and Billings crouched against the outer walls two floors up, trying to avoid ricocheting bullets. At the same time, Fergus jumped in front of the fire door to the foyer and fired off more rounds at Hake and Utting, forcing them to jump back into the lift they'd just stepped out of.

'Let's go,' Danny said, running out of the fire door towards the van.

Hearing all the commotion, Chaz had turned the van around and opened the side door, ready for a quick exit. Holding Amanda's hand, Danny jumped into the back, pulling her on top of him. A second later, Fergus dived in and rolled out of the way for Smudge, who dived in as the van started moving. Chaz revved the van to the max, pumping a cloud of black diesel smoke out of the exhaust as he screeched around to the front of the tower block, sliding the side door shut as they passed the Land

Rovers. Hake and Utting ran out of the tower block, followed by Peeler and Billings and the two officers, watching Chaz's van disappeared around a corner at the end of the street.

'Fuck, bastards!' Peeler yelled, kicking the car tyre.

'Peeler, you'll have to cover this. Utting and I can't get involved. There'll be too many questions about why MI5 agents are on the scene. We've got to get out of here,' Hake said, tucking his gun away and heading for the car with Utting following, clutching a handkerchief to his broken nose.

'Shit, ok, go, go,' Peeler said, pausing for thought before getting on the police radio. 'Control, this Detective Inspector Grant Peeler, we have a 10-57 firearms discharged at 25 Dorchester Place, Paddington. Suspects got away in a red Audi A6, partial plate AP15, last seen heading west on Connaught Street, over,' Peeler said, watching Hake drive away.

'This is control, units dispatched. Are there any casualties, over?'

'No casualties.'

'Ok, Control out.'

Peeler looked at Billings and the two police officers. 'We've got to get our story straight, ok? We had a tip-off about someone dealing on the estate and walked into a drug deal on the back stairs. They were heavily armed and shots were fired before they got away in a red Audi A6. Vague description, right, four guys, hoodies, shades, two black, two white. Got it?'

They all nodded their agreement.

15

Arthur Montgomery's Bentley pulled into a lay-by alongside a long chain-link fence that surrounded Heathrow's cargo terminal. His driver stopped beside a Mercedes AMG GT coupe. Its owner stood in front of the car in a thick winter trench coat, looking through the fence at a cargo plane taxiing onto the runway.

'Good afternoon, Vincent. Is that one of ours?' Arthur said, moving up next to him.

'Yep, fifty tonnes of humanitarian aid bound for Syria and five hundred serial-free L1A1 self-loading rifles and ammunition, officially on the MoD decommission list, courtesy of our military contact,' Vincent Benedict replied without taking his eyes off the plane.

'And the return cargo?' Arthur said matter of fact.

'The Salafi jihadists are ramping up the fighting and are desperate for weapons. They're giving us seventy kilos of pure grade heroin for the rifles.'

'How are we getting it back in?'

'Hidden in sacks of cumin and anise seeds. The sniffer dogs hate the stuff.'

'And if it's discovered?' Arthur said, looking at Vincent.

'The shipping order goes back to a shell company in the Bahamas. No links to you or me, my friend,' Vincent said with a smile.

'You've come a long way since the days of the Wolf, Vincent.'

'Just think how much further we can go once I'm announced as the new Foreign Minister on the eighteenth. Which brings me to our current problem of Miss Wallace and the ex-SAS unit she's been talking to.'

'I'm expecting good news any time now. Mr Hake has tracked her to a flat in Paddington. They should be picking her up as we speak.'

'And the ex-SAS unit?'

'We'll get the woman and her father's notebook and pictures first, then we'll get rid of the unit. Oh, hang on, that's Hake now,' Arthur said, looking at the caller ID on his phone. 'Mr Hake.'

'We didn't get the woman. Pearson and the others showed up out of nowhere. They were heavily armed, we didn't stand a chance. They took the women away with them.'

'I see. This is most unsatisfactory, Mr Hake. Find them,' Arthur said, watching Vincent's face darken as he hung up.

'What the hell has happened now?'

'Pearson and his men grabbed the woman and left,'

Arthur said, a hint of nervousness finally showing on his usually calm façade.

'What do we do now?' Vincent said, in more of a demand than a question.

'We do what we should have done in the first place. We use Special Forces to kill Special Forces and pay Luka and his mercenaries.'

'Agreed. How soon can the Serbians be in the country?'

'They already are,' Arthur said with a certain amount of smugness.

'Good, let's get this over and done with. I'll meet you at the club later,' said Vincent, shaking Arthur's hand before both men split and went back to the warmth of their cars.

'Home please, Roger,' Arthur said, watching Vincent speed away in his Mercedes.

'Very good, sir.'

He waited until they were moving before selecting a number on his phone.

'Yes,' came the Serbians-accented blunt response.

'I would like you to go ahead with the business we discussed.'

'The money,' he replied flatly.

'The deposit will be in your account this afternoon, the rest will be paid on completion, as agreed.'

The line went dead as soon as Arthur stopped talking.

16

'Diggsy, Diggsy, come on, man, open the door,' said Smudge, knocking on the front door of Diggsy's house.

'Go away, Smudge. I don't want anything to do with ya,' came a shout from within.

'Ah come on, man, I didn't know those dudes were going to jump us. Open the door. I need your help.'

'Open the fucking door before I kick it down and shoot you myself,' shouted Chaz, getting impatient behind Smudge.

The locks rattled, and the door opened slowly. Diggsy's face peered around it, his eye black and swollen shut, the side of his face a dark purple colour.

'Alright Diggsy, looking good, my man,' joked Chaz with a big smile as he barged his way past him.

'Got any beers, mate?' Fergus said, following in behind Chaz.

'Guys, don't take the piss. Sorry, mate,' said Smudge, moving inside.

Shaking his head, Diggsy went to shut the door. A hand grabbed it and pushed it back open as Danny held it to one side for Amanda.

'Evening, Diggsy, you wanna put a steak on that eye, mate,' he said, heading after the others

'You lot are taking the fucking piss. Yeah, what do you want?'

'What? Is that all the thanks we get for saving your life?' said Fergus with a hurt look on his face.

'If I didn't know you lot, I wouldn't need bloody saving, would I?' Diggsy said.

'Alright, alright, sorry, mate. Look, Chaz's van is too hot right now. I've put it in the lockup. I need to borrow the magnet,' said Smudge, patting Diggsy on the back while giving him a big grin.

'No, no, no. You're not driving my car. No,' Diggsy said, staring at them with his one open eye while shaking his head.

'Go on, mate, it's just for a day or two. I'll look after it. I'll treat it like it's my own.'

'Yeah, that's what I'm afraid of. No.'

'Ok, fair enough, mate. I guess we'll just have to crash here and hope the gun-toting maniacs don't find us,' said Fergus, swigging one of Diggsy's beers.

Diggsy looked around the room at the bunch of handguns and MP5 submachine guns poking out from underneath their jackets.

'Ah shit,' he said, fishing the keys from his pocket and sliding them across the kitchen table.

'Thanks mate,' Smudge said, scooping them up and

heading for the front door.

'Good man,' said Chaz, patting him on the shoulder on the way out, followed by Fergus, the rest of the beers from Diggsy's fridge under his arm.

'You never saw us,' said Danny, throwing a wad of notes on the table before guiding Amanda out ahead of him.

'I wish fucking hadn't,' Diggsy muttered to himself as the front door slammed behind them.

Outside, they followed Smudge towards the communal car park.

'Why's he call it the magnet, Smudge?' said Chaz.

'Babe magnet, mate,' Smudge said, pressing the unlock button on the key.

There was a pip, and the indicators flashed on a bright orange old Renault 5 Turbo. They stood behind Smudge, taking in the lowered suspension, flames down the side and huge spoiler fixed to the roof at the rear.

'Are you fucking kidding, Smudge?' said Danny.

'What? You said we needed wheels. We've got wheels.'

'Bollocks to it. It's been a rough day. Let's just get in and go,' said Chaz, following Smudge to the car.

Pushing the driver's seat forward, Danny, Chaz and Fergus squeezed into the two-door coupe's tiny rear seat. Amanda got in the front passenger seat before Smudge got in and turned the keys in the ignition. The second the engine fired, the stereo came on with full blast Tupac, the bass deafening from the massive bass bin in the boot.

'Sorry,' said Smudge, turning it off quickly, trying to ignore the three sets of narrowed eyes looking back at him in the rear-view mirror.

'If I could move enough to get this gun out, I'd fucking shoot you myself,' grumbled Chaz.

Ignoring him, Smudge pulled the car out of the car park and down the road towards the factory, the rumbling of the exhaust interrupted by a dump valve letting out a hiss over the turbo whine every time he changed gear.

'Well, this isn't conspicuous at all. How are you holding up?' Danny said to Amanda over the noise.

She turned back in the seat and gave a small nod. 'I'm ok,' she replied, the shock of the events in the tower block still clear in her eyes.

17

Edward headed through the desks and cubicles with a pile of folders under his arm. He stopped next to Hake and Utting's empty desks.

'Lorraine, do you know where Hake and Utting are?' he said to the woman in the cubicle opposite.

'Mr Hake called to say he's taken Utting to hospital. Apparently, he fell down some stairs and broke his nose.'

'Ouch, that sounds painful. Thank you, Lorraine,' Edward said, continuing on his way to his office.

He entered and put the files on his desk. The sight of Simon sitting legs crossed in the chair in the corner made him jump as he turned to close the door.

'Edward,' Simon said, picking a bit of lint off his trousers before fixing him with an unwavering stare.

'Simon, can I get you anything, coffee, tea?' Edward said politely, his finger hovering over the button to call his secretary.

'Tea please, Earl Grey, if you have it,' Simon said, his

voice pleasant as always.

'Yes, Mr Jenkins.'

'Could I have two teas please? Earl Grey,' Edward said over the intercom. 'Now, Simon, to what do I owe the pleasure?'

'I was very rudely interrupted by an acquaintance of ours at my suit fitting today.'

'Oh, and who might that have been?' said Edward, sitting down behind his desk.

'Come now, dear boy, let's not play games. Your breakfast meeting with Paul Greenwood and call to Chief Ryan McGillan indicates you know full well who we are talking about,' Simon said, the room going into silence while Edward's secretary brought a tray with a little pot of Earl Grey, a small jug of milk and dish of sugar next to two bone china cups and saucers. Once she'd left, Simon rose from the chair and moved to the desk. 'Shall I be mother? Milk? Sugar?' He continued pouring the tea.

'Milk and one. Daniel went to Paul after parties unknown paid a drug dealer called Anton to have them killed. This happened after a young lady called Amanda Wallace went to see Daniel about tracking down some arms dealer called the Wolf. Apparently, the Wolf shot her father in Afghanistan then disappeared. Danny's unit arrived shortly after and had him airlifted to hospital. He died en route. Leap forward a few years and his daughter finds a notebook and photos of the Wolf and Danny's SAS unit. What's more concerning is somebody had the crime scenes cleaned up, bodies vanished, crime scenes cleared of evidence. They even sent an email from my office to Police Chief Ryan McGillan telling him MI5 was conducting an active operation and to keep out of the area. Organised, powerful and connected, sound familiar?' Edward said, pausing to sip his tea.

'I see your concern, and I can see why Mr Pearson thought I might be involved. I am not. This leaves you with a more serious problem. You have a mole in the department, and that is something that needs addressing. As for the other items, your drug dealer's full name is Anton Kasovich, Albanian born, nasty piece of work and one of the UK's largest players, with a network of dealers from Lands End to John O'Groats. As for the Wolf, I haven't heard that name mentioned for quite some time. It was widely assumed he'd either been shot in the desert by the Taliban, or got out while he was on top and living it up in Brazil or somewhere similar.'

'They never identified him?'

'No, our Wolf was a very elusive fellow. Now there's a rather important detail that you're missing. Our Mr Wolf didn't trade arms for cash, he traded arms for drugs. Afghanistan heroin, to be precise, and a lot of it. The Taliban were desperate for arms and had bucket loads of heroin. The Wolf took full advantage of that and took ten times the value of drugs to arms for every delivery. What has that got to do with our present problem? Well, it does seem rather coincidental that someone pays the country's number one drug dealer to kill the very people who have the information to identify a prolific and as yet unidentified drug dealer, or should I say drugs supplier,' Simon said, finishing his tea and replacing the cup on the tray.

'You think the Wolf is still active?'

'That's one theory, and if he is, it makes sense he would go to any lengths to keep his identity a secret.'

'What do you suggest we do?'

'Up to you, my dear fellow, but if it were me, I would assist Mr Pearson with any information I might find. Let him run with it for now, see what he uncovers. That way, if it all goes wrong, you have full deniability and if it goes right, the SIS can claim full credit. A win-win, you might say.'

Edward sat digesting the information as Simon got up to leave.

'Goodbye, Edward. I'll be keeping an eye on this one. I'm rather interested in how it will play out,' Simon said with a smug smile before walking briskly out of his office.

18

After a bone shaking journey, Smudge circled the factory, checking for tails or telltale signs that the factory had been compromised. Thankfully, none presented themselves, so he drove in and parked next to Danny's car. Danny, Fergus, and Chaz unfolded themselves from the back seat of the car, straightened up, and headed into the factory. They entered the office block and stripped off their coats and weapons, taking in the warmth of the heaters they'd left running all day.

'Do you want a drink? Are you hungry?' Danny said to Amanda.

'Yes, a coffee please, what food have you got?' she replied, looking white as a sheet and still suffering from a hangover.

'Let's see, Lancashire hotpot, curry, special fried rice,' Danny said, smiling as he rummaged through the remaining microwave meals.

'The hotpot's good,' Chaz chipped in.

'Ok, I'll have that please.'

'Sort that out, Chaz. I'll make a brew,' Danny said, chucking it over to him.

'Right you are, one gourmet meal coming up,' Chaz said, clunking the microwave door shut and tapping the buttons until he heard a reassuring hum.

'May I have a look at your father's things?' Danny said, pointing to Amanda's bag.

'Yes, of course.'

She opened the bag and pulled out a tatty looking old notebook and an envelope. Sliding out a bunch of photos, she put them on the office table.

'Not digital then?'

'No, dad would only use film,' Amanda said with a sad smile.

Opening the notebook at its ribbon, Danny was shocked to find it was David Wallace's last entry, the blood splattered pages showing he wrote it just before Danny and his unit had found him.

'Any idea what it means?' Danny said.

'No, this bit, "HELP came again today" is mentioned several times through the book, always written in capitals.'

Danny read the rest of the page.

"It's him again. The locals call him the Wolf. I'm closer this time. I should be able to get a picture of his face."

Danny stopped reading and picked up the photos, spreading them around the table to get a better look. They showed an old C-27 Spartan cargo plane landing, a truck with armed Afghan Taliban soldiers meeting it. Moving on through the photos, Danny saw a white male with a baseball cap covering most of his sandy-coloured hair, sunglasses covering his eyes as he smiled while he held up a rifle from a crate on the loading door of the aeroplane. It was an over the top million-dollar smile, the sort you'd see on TV when politicians are touting for votes. It was at a fair distance and hard to get detail on the man's face. Danny found a zoomed-in picture. David Wallace had caught the Wolf looking straight at him. Looking at the next picture, it showed the Wolf and Taliban soldiers pointing their weapons in David's direction. Amanda turned away to eat her hotpot, hiding the tears filling her eyes. Danny turned his attention back to the notebook.

"Where are the Special Forces? I told them to be here."

The writing underneath was scratchy and barely legible, obviously written after they had shot him.

"I've got a clear shot of his face. It's him, Fin."

The writing tailed off down the page along with a blood smear. Danny looked at the remaining two pictures. The plane had gone and four military men stood on the dirt airstrip. The last one showed Danny and his unit rushing in David's direction.

'We found him in a hut by the airfield. Chaz managed to keep him alive long enough for the helicopter to evacuate us out of there,' Danny said, picking up the picture of him, Fergus, Chaz and Smudge.

'Thank you for trying,' Amanda said, pulling herself

together.

'This one's good. You can't see his eyes and the hat covers his hair, but you'd still be able to recognise him if you saw him.'

'What about the HELP and it's him, Fin?'

'I don't know, French for finishing or the end. Is it an F? It's hard to tell with the bloodstain. Could be V, Vin, something, or a P for that matter.'

'And the HELP in capitals?'

'HELP International Humanitarian Aid Group,' said Smudge casually as he walked back from the toilets.

'What, Smudge?'

'HELP International Humanitarian Aid Group, you remember them. They were flying aid into the villages all the time we were out there.'

'Well done Smudge. There's me thinking you didn't pay attention while we were out there,' Danny said with a grin.

'Hidden talents mate, I'm always underestimated.'

'So what do we do now?' Amanda said, her enthusiasm picking up at the sign of progress.

'We have to find out who this scum Anton is and pay him a visit. Someone paid him a lot of money to get kill us and I want to know who.'

'How do we find out who Anton is?' said Amanda.

'Anton Kasovich, they reckon he's responsible for seventy percent of all the drugs in the UK. He's clever though, never gets his hands dirty, lives in a bloody great place in Wimbledon,' Smudge said, casually walking back past them before sitting down with a brew.

Danny, Chaz, Fergus, and Amanda all turned around and stared at him.

'What? Well, that's what Diggsy's uncle's next-door neighbour said, and he's been inside for drug dealing more times than he's been out.'

'And you didn't think to share this little nugget of information with us sooner?' said Danny, looking at him in disbelief.

'It only just occurred to me. Anyway, if you're going to take the piss, I won't bother helping you anymore.'

'I don't suppose you know where in Wimbledon he lives?'

'Yeah, big gaff at the end of Wool Road, backs onto the Royal Wimbledon Golf Course. Me and Diggsy took some old bedroom furniture away from the house next door. A couple of big fuckers came out of the gate and told us to move the van away from his property. I think they thought we were undercover fuzz.'

All eyes stared at Smudge again until Danny finally looked at his watch, nearly six o'clock.

'Drink up, Smudge. You and me are going to go and scope this house out. Chaz, Fergus, check the weapons and ammo situation. Amanda, you'll be safe here with Fergus and Chaz. I'll only be an hour or so.'

'Yes, boss,' said Chaz, stripping an MP5, glad to be doing something rather than nothing.

19

After finding nothing of use at Danny's house, Luka and his men had moved on.

'There's nothing here. Let's go,' said Luka, walking out of Smudge's turned-upside-down living room.

His three men fell in behind him from the kitchen and upstairs; big men, fit men, not fit like you go to the gym fit, fit like elite military fit; short haircuts, their eyes taking in their surroundings as they moved with the confidence of men who could take anything thrown at them. They moved towards a Mercedes G-Class 4x4, its rugged square shape looking more suited to rough terrain than the wintery streets of inner London. Luka paused just before getting in. He turned slowly and eyed the tatty blue Luton van with Smith & Diggs Removals and House Clearance written above a mobile number in uneven, sticky letters. He walked up to the passenger door, glanced up and down the deserted road before pulling out a handgun and cracking the window hard with the butt. It shattered into a million pieces, allowing Luka to reach in and pull the door release. Undeterred by the internal light coming on, Luka rifled through the bits of paper on the dash before opening the glove box. Under the sweet wrappers and woolly hat, he found the registration document for the vehicle with Terence Diggs' name and an address on it. A smile curled on the corner of Luka's mouth as he put the document in his pocket, shut the door, and walked back to the Mercedes. He climbed into the passenger seat and handed the document to the driver.

'We go here,' he said.

'Ok,' the driver said, pulling away.

They drove the short distance to the other side of the housing estate before pulling up outside Diggsy's house.

***

'Yeah, yeah, I'm coming. That better be you bringing my car back, Smudge,' said Diggsy, swinging the door open without thinking.

Four men stared back at him, expressionless, hard, scary faces, with cold, alert eyes.

'Mr Diggs, I'm trying to find a friend of yours, Darren Smith,' Luka said, smiling to show a gold front tooth.

'I don't know any Smith, pal, so I can't help you,' Diggsy said, swinging the door shut.

Luka's hand slammed on the wood, forcing the door back open with ease. He walked forward into the hall with his three men following close behind as a terrified Diggsy backed into the kitchen.

'I think we start this again, yes,' Luka said in broken English, his hand sliding inside his jacket to pull a six-inch ornate hunting knife out. Its handmade Damascus steel glinted under the harsh fluorescent lighting. 'You know, this was my father's knife. It's very special to me. It's seen much blood, maybe it will see yours. Now, where are Mr Smith and his friends?'

20

'D.I. Peeler, what brings you down to the murky world of traffic?'

'I need a favour Martin, I need you to look for a vehicle for me,' said Peeler, passing a piece of paper with the number plate and description of Diggsy's car on it.

'Priority?' Martin said, typing the plate into London's Automatic Number Plate Recognition system, ANPR for short.

'Call it a personal favour,' Peeler said, tucking a wad of twenty-pound notes into Martin's desk tidy.

Martin plucked the cash out quickly, sliding it into his pocket, looking nervously around the room to make sure nobody saw.

'Good boy, call me the second you get anything,' Peeler said, patting Martin on the back before walking casually out of the traffic department.

***

'We nearly there, Smudge?' Danny said over the noise of the exhaust.

'Yeah, should be just, er, yep there it is, next left,' Smudge said, pointing at the turning.

Danny turned down Wool Road and followed the tree-lined road past all the large houses toward Anton Kasovich's, the road getting icier as they got closer to the dead end. The earlier snow had turned to slush as the day went on and was now turning to ice as the evening temperature sank below zero.

'That's the one with the wall and electric gates,' Smudge said as they approached.

Danny stopped short. Looking at the imposing front of the property, he looked at the house next door. No lights on, but a camera and floodlights attached to the front of the garage, aiming at the front door and drive.

'Ok Smudge, this is what I want you to do.'

***

'Yeah?'

'Hi, it's Martin. I've just had a hit on your vehicle. It just turned off the A3 onto the A238, heading into Wimbledon on Copse Hill Road. I don't know exactly where it went from there, but it hasn't appeared on the cameras heading out of the area, so it must be somewhere in the housing estates either side of Copse Hill Road between the A238 and Ridgeway.'

'Thanks, Martin, keep an eye out for it. Call me immediately if it leaves the area, ok?' said Peeler, talking quietly as he walked out of the station.

'Ok, will do.'

Looking towards the car, he grabbed the attention of Stewart Billings and pointed towards the exit to the police yard while he dialled another number.

'Talk.'

'The car is somewhere in a housing estate off Copse Hill Road, Wimbledon. We're on our way there now,' said Peeler as Billings pulled the car up beside him.

'If you find it, you call me and keep out of our way,' Luka replied bluntly, before hanging up.

'He's a fucking charmer, that one. Head for Wimbledon, Stew,' said Peeler, shutting the car door.

***

Moving through the shrubs, Danny stayed close to the wall to avoid the sensor kicking the floodlights on in Anton's neighbour's house. He stopped when he was out of sight in the darkness down the side of the house and waited for his cue. A couple of minutes later, he heard the rumble as Smudge fired up Diggsy's car and drove it forward until it sat outside the automatic gates of Anton's house.

One, two, three.

Danny jumped up, grabbed the top of the wall, and hung there.

Seven, eight, nine.

On the count of ten, Smudge revved the car up, its exhaust cracking and popping as the turbo whined and dump valve let out loud hisses. Danny pulled himself up far enough to see over the top. The house was huge, with a large circular drive at the front and lit-up patio and swimming pool to the rear, followed by a long landscaped garden backing onto the thirteenth hole of the Royal Wimbledon Golf Course.

Glancing to the front, Danny watched three big men come out of the house and head for the gate and Smudge's racket outside. As the gate started to slide smoothly open, Danny pulled himself up before dropping down into a flower bed on the other side. He stayed still, crouching in the dark. No one came running, and the three guys were still preoccupied with Smudge.

'Hey, move that piece of shit,' one guy yelled in an Eastern European accent.

'Alright, mate, keep your hair on, the clutch is playing up, I can't get it in gear,' Smudge shouted out the window while revving the hell out of the engine while pushing the gear lever gently forward, without pushing the clutch down, to make a horrible grinding sound.

Running across to the rear corner, Danny peeped around to the back of the house. With no one there, he edged forward until he could see in through the long row of bi-folding doors that would open up in summer to make the best use of the kitchen-cum-lounge, patio and pool area. A leggy blonde in sports lycra was working out to Joe Wicks on a massive wall-mounted TV, while one of Anton's men stood in the kitchen working his eyeballs out on her arse as she bent over. The man jumped and looked away like he'd had an electric shock when another guy walked into the kitchen shouting at a muscle-bound giant behind him.

I guess you're Anton.

It was hard to hear what they were saying, but from the snippets he got through the thick double glazing, Anton was seriously pissed off by the racket Smudge was making out the front. The big guy and the arse fan both pulled Russian-made MP-446 handguns out and headed towards the front door.

Time to go.

Danny spun back around to the side of the house and darted back in the darkness to the flowerbed by the wall. After popping up and over, he made his way back to the road fifty metres up from Anton's house.

'I won't tell you again. Get this piece of shit away from the house.'

'Yeah, I'm trying,' Smudge yelled back with one eye on the mirror and the other on the two characters coming out the house with handguns.

Thankful to see Danny's shadow appear on the pavement a little way behind him. Smudge threw it into first and spun the car around on the icy road. 'It's alright, you ugly bastards, I've got it now,' Smudge shouted out the open window as he spun the car away.

The three hard-looking men glared after Smudge, turning back towards the house as he sped away.

'Who was that?' the big guy growled.

'Nobody, just some idiot with car trouble,' one of the others said, moving back towards the house as the electric gates closed smoothly behind him.

21

'Turn the heater up, Smudge,' Danny said, rubbing his hands from the cold as he got in the car a little way up from Anton's.

'Ok, how did you get on?'

'Doesn't look too bad, five guys, light sidearms. If we go in after they've all gone to bed, it should be a doddle.'

'Best way in?' Smudge said, turning onto Copse Hill Road.

'Cut across the golf course behind the house, hop over the wall and approach the house from the back, split into two teams and zip-tie the heavies up before we have a word with this Anton bloke.'

'Sounds good to—'

The back window exploding inwards in a shower of glass crystals cut Smudge short. Three bullets passed between him and Danny at supersonic speed, punching neat little round holes in the laminated front windscreen as they exited the vehicle. Reacting on instinct rather than thought, Smudge slammed the Renault 5 Turbo down a gear and floored the accelerator, launching the little car forward, snaking it along the slippery tarmac as the tyres fought for grip. Twisting in his seat, Danny reached into the rear footwell and grabbed an MP5 submachine gun. He stared out the glassless rear window at Luka revving the powerful Mercedes G-Class 4x4 after them. One of Luka's men had his head and shoulders out of the front passenger window, struggling to keep his AK47 steady as he stared down the sights at the Renault. On the other side of the Mercedes, another man leaned out the rear passenger window, his arms locked as he aimed a handgun at them.

'Get us out of here, Smudge,' Danny said, sliding down low in the seat as bullets punched through the thin bodywork, embedding themselves into the wood of the heavy subwoofer that filled the boot space.

'Roger that,' Smudge shouted over the noise, handbrake-turning the little car off the main road into a quiet Wimbledon housing estate.

Luka took the more direct approach, bouncing the all-terrain vehicle up the kerb and crashing it through a little picket fence in an explosion of white painted wood as he ploughed through someone's front garden, cutting the corner in his pursuit.

'Who the fuck are these guys?' Smudge shouted over the screaming engine.

'They're not Anton's men, or they would have gone for us at the house.'

'Well, they're seriously pissed off about something.'

Trying to hold the rifle steady between the seats, Danny let off a short burst of fire, forcing one man back inside as bullets sparked off the Mercedes' bodywork, shattering the driver's side wing mirror as Luka swerved to get out of the line of fire.

'Smudge!' Danny shouted, watching the man slide his weapon back out the window.

'Alright, alright, I'm moving,' Smudge shouted, sliding the Renault around a sharp corner, dodging a burst of fire that continued on its journey before bursting through the living room window of the house on the corner, destroying the flatscreen TV on the wall opposite as a group of lads watched a violent gun battle in the film John Wick 3. They sat open-mouthed in shock, cans of beer in hand as they stared at the smouldering screen.

'Hold on,' shouted Smudge, accelerating down a road lined with terraced houses. The owners' cars parked bumper to bumper on either side of them as they sped recklessly down the narrow gap in the middle.

Looking behind them, Danny watched as the wide Mercedes accelerated after them, obliterating the wing mirrors of the parked cars on either side as it closed the gap. The only good thing was the narrow gap forced the gunmen inside the car. Turning forward, everything whizzed by in a blur as they approached eighty miles an hour.

'Watch out!' Danny yelled as someone pushed their car door open to get out.

Smudge hit the door at full speed, ripping it off its hinges as the Renault's headlight exploded and the front corner of the car crumpled. Smudge instinctively hit the brakes to slow down and keep the car under control, the Mercedes rammed them from behind, pushing them straight towards a house on the other side of a T-junction directly ahead of them.

'You'll have to punch it, or he'll ram us into the house,' shouted Danny.

'Hold on,' Smudge shouted back, dropping it down a gear and flooring the accelerator.

The turbo kicked in and the Renault moved away from the Mercedes just enough for Smudge to pull the handbrake and feather the throttle, drifting the car around the T-junction, bouncing the rear end off a parked car before straightening up and speeding away. Luka's Mercedes was too close and too heavy to take the corner. Its brakes locked up as it slid straight across the junction, bursting through a low garden wall before embedding itself into the bay window of the terraced house behind. Luka and his men disappeared from view in a cloud of exploding airbags.

'Fuck!' Luka yelled, pulling his hunting knife out as the airbag deflated. He cut it free of the steering wheel and ground the car into reverse, revving it hard to pull it out of the rubble and back onto the road. The owners of the house came rushing through from the kitchen, only to be left staring through the hole in their living room at Luka and his men as they sped off down the road.

Several streets ahead Smudge continued to take lefts and rights through the estate while Danny kept a check behind to make sure they'd lost them.

'How the hell did they find us?' Smudge said, slowing down to the speed limit.

'They must have tracked the car. You remember the men in the tower block with Police on their vests?'

'Yeah, but how did they know what we were driving?' Smudge said, the answer dawning on him the moment he said it. 'Oh shit, Diggsy! Fuck, we've gotta go check on him,' Smudge said, driving the car as fast as it would go.

'Alright, Smudge, take it easy, mate. We'll check on Diggsy, but we need to ditch this car first.'

22

After dumping Diggsy's car in Battersea, Danny and Smudge took the underground to Greenwich and headed for Danny's best friend Scott Miller's penthouse apartment overlooking the Thames.

'Evening, Daniel and, er, Darren, isn't it?' said Scott at his front door after buzzing them into the building.

'Alright, Scotty boy. I've got a little favour to ask you,' said Danny, taking a submachine gun out from under his jacket and popping it down on the seat next to him, the two Glock 17s in his shoulder holsters coming into view as his jacket flapped open when he was sitting down.

'Do you ever just have a normal day? Tea, coffee? Something stronger perhaps?' Scott said without batting an eyelid.

'I'll take a beer if you have one,' said Smudge.

'Nothing for me, mate,' said Danny, giving his friend a weary smile.

'Ok, one beer coming up,' said Scott, heading for the fridge.

'Now, about this favour,' Scott said, handing Smudge a beer and having one for himself.

'I need to borrow a car.'

'Which one, old boy?' Scott said, unfazed by the question.

'I don't know. How many have you got now?' Danny said in surprise.

'Er, let me see, there's the Porsche 718 Cayman GT4 RS, the Audi RS5, a BMW XB7, and a rather nice little Tesla thingamabob. There's the vintage E-type Jag, but you're not borrowing that one. If you're looking for space, the XB7's probably your best bet. It's the Alpine model, 4.4 litre twin turbo, 612 horsepower, quite a lively little devil.'

'Are you sure you can spare it, mate? I wouldn't want to leave you having to walk to the shops,' Danny said with a chuckle.

'Ha ha, very funny. I can see you're in some sort of trouble. Of course you can borrow it. Although, I would very much appreciate it if you can return it in one piece.'

'Thanks, Scott, you're the best, mate,' Danny said, getting up to leave.

'Mmm, well, I know you'd do the same for me. Be careful, dear boy,' Scott said, handing the keys over.

'Always am, Scotty boy. Oh, probably best if you don't mention this to your sister.'

'Mum's the word, old man.'

Both of them ignored the lift and made their way

down the stairs to the underground car park.

'Jesus, just how rich is Scott?' Smudge said, shaking his head at Scott's array of luxury sports cars sitting in his bay.

'Pretty rich, Smudge, fair play to him. He's earned every penny of it.'

'Is his sister rich? Is that why you're going out with her?' Smudge said with a cheeky grin.

'No mate, she's skint, especially after I blew up her boss's business and set her house on fire with some bloke's head,' Danny said, getting in the big BMW.

'Er, what?' Smudge said as the words sunk in.

'Don't go there. Let's check on Diggsy.'

With that, Danny started the car, smiling at the throaty rumble of exhaust as he drove it up and out of the underground car park before heading for Wandsworth.

They coasted down the road slowly, checking out the cars on the road and the dark and quiet front of Diggsy's house. Nothing out of the ordinary, no dented Mercedes full of armed men. Carrying on down the road, Danny turned left, crawling through the estate, turning left again and again until they came back down Diggsy's road. It was still quiet, so he pulled into the nearest space and turned the engine and lights off. They sat in the dark for five minutes, both men checking their surroundings without saying a word.

'Here we go,' Danny said, pulling both of his Glocks out and handing one to Smudge.

They got out, Danny heading for the front door while

Smudge walked backwards behind him, his eyes flicking across the road to the houses opposite. When he reached the front door, Danny put his ear against its surface, no sound and no lights showing through the narrow frosted glass panel. Backing up, Danny got ready to kick the lock open.

'Whoa, whoa, hang on, mate,' Smudge said, moving in front of him to lift the door mat and pick up a shiny front door key.

'Really?' Danny said, shaking his head.

Smudge put the key in the lock, opened the door, and went inside. Danny took a last look around, then followed him, clicking the door shut behind him.

The house was quiet. Within a few seconds, Danny and Smudge knew Diggsy was dead. The earthy, rusty smell of blood, a lot of blood, hung in the air. Alien to some, but memory-evoking to Danny and Smudge, they moved slowly down the hall and pushed the kitchen door open. Danny felt for the light switch and flicked the harsh fluorescent light on. Diggsy sat cable tied to a chair in the middle of a large puddle of his own blood. His shirt was off with his belly sliced wide open, letting his intestines unravel into a heap between his legs. Their eyes moved up the body to see Diggsy's throat cut from ear to ear.

'Fucking bastard, fuck. What the hell did that poor sod ever do to anyone?' Smudge said, anger on his face as he turned away.

Danny looked at the body, the ties, and the bloody floor.

'That's it. I'm gonna do that fucking bastard Anton and his fucking mob. I'm gonna blow his fucking bollocks off and watch him bleed to death,' said Smudge through gritted teeth.

'I don't think this was Anton's lot,' Danny said, turning to leave.

'What, you don't?'

'Nah, Anton's men were amateur hour: gaffer tape, fists and trainers,' Danny said, his hand pausing by the light switch.

'Huh? What do you mean?'

'This is cable ties, hands and feet, and torture by men who know how to do it. Lastly, they wore boots, military, like men of habit,' Danny said, pointing to the four sets of bloody boot prints on the tiled floor.

'Shit, I don't like the sound of that.'

'Neither do I, Smudge. Let's go,' Danny said, flicking the light off, plunging Diggsy's body into darkness.

23

'Can I get you anything else, gentlemen?' said Leonard, clearing Vincent Benedict and Arthur Montgomery's table at the Lansdowne Club.

'A brandy would go down nicely please, Leonard,' said Arthur.

'Scotch on the rocks,' Vincent said, giving him his best politician smile.

'Very good, sirs,' Leonard said, whisking the empty plates away.

'So they got away again,' Vincent said, his face dropping to show his annoyance the second Leonard left.

'I'm afraid so,' Arthur answered, unfazed as usual.

'Where did you say they were when Luka's men spotted them?'

'Er, Wimbledon, coming out of the houses that back onto the golf course.'

Vincent's face turned into a frown as he leant across

the table.

'Anton Kasovich's house backs onto the golf course,' he said in a low growl.

'Ah, that does put a new dimension on our problem,' Arthur said, his face dropping for the first time.

'A new fucking dimension. If Pearson's lot have figured out it was Anton's men who attacked them, they'll be going for him next, and guess what, Arthur? If they get to Anton, he'll lead them straight to us,' said Vincent, trying to talk as quietly as he could through his growing anger.

'So what do you suggest we do?' Arthur replied without reacting to Vincent's outburst.

'We burn Anton. Get Luka to do it. Now. Tonight.'

'It'll cost a fortune. Distribution will be broken, and every scummy dealer from here to Edinburgh will try to take a piece of the action.'

'Not if we switch to the Asian. He can take over distribution and has the men to hold our ground. Anyway, what choice do we have? If Pearson gets to Anton and my name gets linked to Wallace's pictures and notes, we're finished.'

Arthur and Vincent sat back as Leonard appeared with the drinks. They sat staring at each other until Leonard left.

'Ok, agreed,' said Arthur, taking a big gulp of his brandy before making the call.

***

Moving through Chaz's house, Luka headed into the

office. He rifled through the drawers and invoices, looking for any clue to their whereabouts. He was thumbing through a work diary when his phone rang.

'Yes.'

'It's me. I have an urgent job for you.'

'I already have urgent job,' Luka said coldly.

'Yes, I know, but this one is more important. Once it's done, you can continue with the current contract.'

'What is job?' Luka said in his thick Serbian accent, his eyes falling on Chaz's wall planner and pin board as he talked.

'I need you to go to a house in Wimbledon and kill someone. Just kill them and whoever's in the house and leave.'

'Money,' Luka said, more of a demand than a question.

'Your usual fee will be in your account within the hour.'

'I want an extra thirty thousand for the urgency,' Luka said, moving closer to the planner.

'Ok, agreed, I'll send you the address and a photo of the target,' Arthur said, after a short pause.

Luka hung up and slid the phone into his pocket. He reached out his hand and unpinned a picture of a derelict factory and an order for a demolition survey from a Derick Leman to Charles Leman.

'We go,' he said to the others, folding the picture and paperwork, putting them in his pocket.

His phone buzzed as they left the house and climbed into the dented Mercedes. Luka looked at the photo of

Anton and then the address before starting the car up and heading for Wimbledon.

24

'Hey where have you two been? I was starting to get worried,' Chaz said, seeing Danny and Smudge walk back into the office.

'We had car trouble,' Danny said, clearly in a bad mood.

'Yeah, what sort of trouble?' said Fergus, looking up from his makeshift bed.

'A big Mercedes full of armed crazy bastards sort of trouble,' said Smudge, looking equally pissed off.

'Shit, more of Anton's men?'

'I don't think so, hard-looking bastards. I'm guessing ex-military, mercenaries,' said Danny, dumping the MP5 on the table.

'They killed Diggsy,' Smudge added, slumping into a chair.

'Bloody hell, sorry, Smudge,' said Fergus.

'Are you alright?' Danny said, seeing Amanda's frightened face looking back at him.

She managed an unconvincing smile back.

'Right, guys, let's get our shit together. We're going to hit Anton Kasovich's place before dawn and catch them napping. We'll find out who gave him the order to kill us, and hopefully find out who this Wolf character is as well,' Danny said, checking how many bullets were left in the rifle after their gun fight with the Mercedes.

'Roger that,' said Chaz.

'Yes, boss,' Fergus chipped in.

Smudge gave a thumbs up from his seat.

'Ok, it's just coming up to ten. Get some grub and grab a couple of hours' kip. We'll hit them at 3 a.m.'

The group nodded their agreement.

'What do I do?' said Amanda timidly.

'You stay here where it's safe,' Danny said more forcibly than he intended.

'No, no, I don't want to stay here on my own. What if none of you come back? What do I do then?'

'Whoa, ok, ok, sorry, take it easy. You can come with us and wait in the car with Smudge,' Danny said reassuringly, while waiting for Smudge to complain about being left in the car.

'Thank you,' she said, relaxing a little.

Smudge was about to complain, but held it in. He knew Danny was right to keep him away from Anton's. He was too emotional over Diggsy's death, and being emotional on a job, got people killed.

They did as Danny said, topping up on food and hot drinks before catching a couple of hours' sleep. At 2 a.m, Danny moved around and gave everyone a shake. As they got up, they saw hot mugs of coffee sitting on the table for each of them.

'Thanks, mum,' Fergus said, wiping the sleep out of his eyes.

Half an hour later, all five of them climbed into Scott's BMW XB7 and headed through the deserted streets towards Wimbledon. They took the turning before the one leading to Anton's house and followed it to the end, parking up alongside a hedge that divided the cul-de-sac from The Royal Wimbledon Golf Club.

'Ok, Smudge, keep Miss Wallace company. We'll be back in less than thirty minutes. If it's looking like longer to get Anton to talk, we'll bag him and take him back to the factory for interrogation,' Danny said, getting out.

'Roger that, boss.'

Finding the thinnest part of the hedge, Danny, Chaz and Fergus pushed their way through, ignoring the twigs and bramble thorns that snagged their clothes. They emerged in the rough by the fairway of hole 13.

'This way,' Danny said, barely visible against the hedge as he followed it up towards Anton's house. 'This is it.'

Pushing through a line of conifers, Danny came out by the wall at the bottom of Anton's garden.

'Ladies first,' Fergus said, leaning his back against the wall and linking his hands together to give a leg up.

Danny put his foot in Fergus's hands, grabbed the top of the wall, and hopped up to sit astride the wall. Chaz popped up next, sitting facing Danny as the two of them reached an arm down and hauled Fergus up. They sat in the darkness looking up the garden at the house, its downstairs lights still burning through the large expanse of bi-folding doors.

'What do you reckon?' said Chaz.

'Don't know. I can't see anyone moving. Perhaps they leave them on all night,' Danny said, trying to shake off the growing feeling of unease.

'Well, we ain't going to find out sitting here,' said Fergus, dropping down into the garden.

Danny and Chaz dropped down beside him, swinging the MP5's up from the strap over their shoulders. Following the wall, they hurried up the garden, crossing to the rear of the house when they got level with the pool. Flattened against the brickwork, the three of them edged towards the bi-folding doors. Darting his head across, Danny took a quick look into the kitchen.

'All clear,' he whispered.

Letting the MP5 swing down on the shoulder strap, he pulled a little leather pouch from his pocket and slid two lock picks out. Crossing and dropping to his knees by the door, Danny reached in towards the lock, pausing short when he realised the door was already ajar. He slid the lock picks away and swung the MP5 up, opening the door slowly to enter with Chaz and Fergus moving in closely behind him.

25

'Something's not right here,' whispered Fergus as they fanned out and moved into the room. He stopped dead by the kitchen island. Anton's right-hand man, Kovak, lay behind it in a pool of blood, his torso riddled with bullet holes from automatic fire. Throwing his hand up, Fergus stopped Danny and Chaz dead in their tracks. He pointed to his eyes, then put one finger up and drew it across his throat to indicate eyes on one dead. Danny swung his head to Chaz to see him show that Anton's girlfriend and the man who'd been staring at her arse were dead behind the dining room table. Looking at the floor, Danny caught sight of boot prints on the white marble tiles, military boots, all the same make.

The bastards are cleaning house.

The three of them moved into the hall and started a sweep, falling into an unspoken pattern of cover and entry as if they'd never left the SAS. They found more bodies as they went, eventually finding Anton face down in a puddle of blood in the master bedroom.

'Jesus, give us a fucking break,' Danny said, turning Anton over, feeling for a pulse on the slim chance he might be still alive. 'He's still warm.'

'Yeah and you can smell the gun discharge, we must have missed them by minutes,' said Fergus.

Danny was about to get up when something under the bed caught his eye. He reached under and pulled out a phone and a business card for the Lansdowne Club.

'He must have been holding this when they shot him,' Danny said, spinning the card over in his fingers to reveal 11AM and a mobile number written on the back.

'Any idea what it means?' said Chaz.

'No mate,' said Danny, kneeling back down to put Anton's thumb on the phone to unlock it.

He went into the menu and turned the thumb and pin locks off for the phone, then looked at the call log.

'He called that number fifteen minutes ago.'

'Probably when he realised he'd been double-crossed,' said Chaz.

'You could be right,' said Danny, pressing redial.

It rang for a frustratingly long time before it clicked and the display counted the seconds of the answered call. Nobody said a word, but he could hear someone breathing on the other end of the phone, a little fast, a little nervous.

'I'm coming for you,' Danny growled in a low, menacing voice.

The phone clicked, and the line went dead.

***

In his six-bedroom townhouse in the affluent St John's Wood area of London, Arthur put the phone down on his office desk and stared at it. His calm, always in control demeanour was well and truly shaken by the menace in Danny's voice. The call from Anton fifteen minutes ago, swearing and threatening down the phone just before Luka and his men cut him down, hadn't raised an eyebrow, but the chilling, real threat from a man like Pearson was not to be taken lightly. He composed himself after a minute or so and picked the phone up again.

'Pearson is at Anton's.'

'It is of no consequence. We are ready for him.'

'Good. This phone is compromised. I'll text you a new number in a minute. Call me when it's done.'

The phone went dead without a response, as usual. Arthur took the battery and sim out before snapping it and dumping them in the bin. He pulled the desk drawer open and picked up another pay as you go phone, powered it up and text the number to Luka. Once done, Arthur sat back in his leather office chair, all thoughts of going to bed and sleep pushed far from his mind.

***

'That'll rattle him,' said Chaz.

'Yeah, it gave me chills. You're a scary guy, do you know that?' said Fergus with a grin.

'Shut up, you idiots,' Danny said, smiling back. 'Come on, let's get out of here. We'll figure out what to do next when we're back at the factory.'

They left the way they came, treading carefully, touching nothing. Chaz gave the back door a quick rub down to make sure they'd left no prints behind. A few minutes later, they dragged themselves back through the hedge, making Amanda jump as they emerged next to the car.

'That was quick. How did it go?' said Smudge, turning the car around before driving quietly out of the cul-de-sac.

'Badly, they're all dead,' said Danny, without emotion.

'What, you killed them all?'

'No mate, our friends with the boots got there first and cleaned house.'

'What do we do now?' said Smudge.

'I don't know Smudge. I need time to think. Just get us back to the factory, mate,' Danny said, closing his eyes as a wave of exhaustion washed over him.

Half an hour later, he woke with a start. Smudge was turning through the gate that led to the factory.

'Did you go around the block and check the area?' he said, sitting up fully awake.

'Nah, it's half four in the morning. Look, it's all quiet.'

Danny's senses were on full alert. His eyes darted across the factory. There was something wrong, but he just couldn't put his finger on it. Danny looked at the tracks in the snow. They looked the same. Wait, no. A set of tyre tracks peeled off from the ones they'd made earlier, disappearing around the back of the factory. His eyes darted back to the building. It had plenty of broken panes of glass, but now there were two more.

'Get us out of here now, Smudge. Go, go, go!' he yelled.

Smudge reacted quickly, spinning the car to get back out the gate. As the back of the car came around, bursts of automatic fire broke the early morning silence. The factory windows lit up with muzzle flashes, and the rear window of the car imploded. The bodywork shook as bullets ripped into it in a hail of metallic pings.

'Argh, fuck, I'm hit,' yelled Fergus in shock and pain.

Smudge punched the accelerator, kicking all 612 horsepower of the 4.4 litre twin turbo engine to the four-wheel drive. The car snaked before finding grip and propelled them out the gate like a freshly launched rocket.

'Stay with us, Ferg. Smudge, get us to St Thomas' A&E. NOW!' Danny yelled.

26

'Amanda, slide over me so I can check Fergus. Amanda,' Chaz said, turning the light on above them and talking firmly to cut through her shock.

She finally nodded and slid over him, allowing Chaz to unzip Fergus's jacket and check the wound.

'Chaz?' Danny ordered from the front.

'The bullet's gone through the side. I think it's below the ribs. Shit, he's losing a lot of blood,' Chaz said, putting pressure on the wound.

'Smudge?'

'Seven minutes, boss.'

'Make it five.'

'Roger that,' Smudge said, pushing the car insanely fast through London's suburban streets.

'Ferg, you still with us, pal?' Chaz said.

'Where the hell else would I be?' Fergus grunted back, gasping in pain.

'Good man. When we get there, I'll take him in. You

guys get off quick before the police turn up,' said Chaz, looking at Danny in the front.

He wanted to argue, but knew it had to be done. If they dumped Fergus outside, he might bleed out before they got to him.

'Ok, when the police take you in for questioning, stall them, say nothing, you know nothing, ok? Trust me, I'll get you out,' Danny said, twisting around in his seat to see Chaz, with Fergus next to him shaking as his body went into shock.

'Smudge,' Danny yelled.

'We're here,' Smudge shouted, cornering hard into the ambulance drop off bay.

Danny leaped out of the car and ran to Fergus's door, he opened it and slid his arm around him, Fergus groaned in pain as Danny lifted him up and out of the slippery blood-soaked seat, a bullet hole visible in the soft leather behind him. Chaz left his guns in the car and slid out to take Fergus off Danny's hands.

'I've got him, go, quickly. The second I walk in there with a gunshot wound, the Met's armed response unit will be on their way.'

'Alright, Chaz. Hang in there, Ferg,' Danny said, leaving them to get back in the car. 'Get us out of here, Smudge.'

Hitting the accelerator, Smudge launched the car out of the hospital and away. A couple of miles down the road, they slowed down and started zigzagging through the back streets away from traffic cameras and police patrols.

'Please tell me you didn't leave the pictures and notebook back at the factory when we went to Anton's,' Danny said, turning in his seat to look at Amanda.

'Oh god, I'm sorry, I'm so sorry,' she replied, moving her hand up and wincing at Fergus's blood dripping off it.

'Shit,' Danny shouted, before quickly regaining composure, 'It's ok, it's not your fault, don't worry, we're still going to get this bastard.'

'Where are we heading, boss?' Smudge said.

'Richmond, I've got to see Edward Jenkins. I need him to get Chaz out of custody and make sure Ferg is safe in hospital.'

'Richmond it is then.'

***

'Can I get some help here?' Chaz yelled, entering the A&E department.

Doctors and staff ran over with a trolley at the sight of Chaz holding Fergus up as he fell into unconsciousness in his arms, his torso soaked in blood.

'What happened?' the doctor asked as they put Fergus on the trolley.

'Gunshot wound, 9mm. Entry point lower left-hand side, exit wound front abdomen. Happened fifteen minutes ago, I applied pressure, but he's lost a lot of blood. He's type O-negative,' Chaz said calmly.

'Are you a doctor?'

'No, forces medic, ex-military,' Chaz said, already aware of the receptionist talking quickly on the phone, her eyes flicking nervously between him and the entrance door.

'Ok, we'll take him from here. I need you to stay in reception,' the doctor said, wheeling Fergus off between two hospital security staff.

Chaz turned towards the exit to see two more security staff blocking his way. By the time he'd contemplated taking them out and leaving, police cars flew into the bay outside with armed response officers pouring out, front and back. Chaz calmly went down on his knees and dropped on his front before placing his hands on the back of his head.

'Armed police, stay down, don't move!' yelled multiple voices before two knelt on his back to cuff him and another patted him down for weapons.

Chaz said nothing. He just relaxed and let them bundle him in the back of a police car and whisk him away.

27

'Next left, Smudge,' Danny said, his hands close to the heater vent as he tried to keep the sub-zero cold out as it curled in through the shot-out rear window.

'Are we nearly there?' said Amanda, leaning forward between the two front seats to get out of the icy blast.

'Yeah, he lives on the next street over.'

Smudge took the left turn and jumped on the brakes. Thirty metres ahead of him were two police cars pulled across the road, blocking their path. Armed police officers in tactical gear pointed MP5 submachine guns over the bonnets at them.

Throwing it in reverse, Smudge yelled, 'Move,' to Amanda as he swung his head around to look through the glassless rear window.

The powerful car lurched backwards, only getting a few metres before two more police cars skidded to a halt behind them, blocking the turning out of the road. More armed police hurried out of the vehicles, taking up positions behind them, guns pointed at the ready.

Smudge stamped on the brake again, leaving them sitting halfway between the police cars.

'Turn the engine off, Smudge. We've got nowhere to go. Amanda, we're going to get out now. Just open the door and get out slowly with your hands up. There'll be a lot of shouting, it's just their training, ok? Just do as they say and it'll all be fine,' Danny said, looking at her face all lit up by strobing blue lights to give her a reassuring smile.

'What's going to happen to us?' she said.

'They'll arrest us, then separate us. Don't worry, ok? Look at me, I'll sort it. Ready Smudge?'

'As I'll ever be,' Smudge said, pulling the handle and opening the door slowly before showing his hands, palms up.

'Keep your hands where we can see them and get down on your knees,' came multiple shouts, bright torches in their faces blinding them as the officers approached with their guns trained on Danny, Smudge and Amanda's faces.

'Place your hands on the floor and get down on your front, NOW.'

The three of them complied. Police knelt on their backs and pulled their arms behind them to secure them in handcuffs. While other officers pulled Danny and Smudge's handguns from their holsters, a black panel van pulled up beside them. Its back doors opened to show four square cages with a seat in each. The police pulled them to their feet and guided them inside, sitting them down and fixing their cuffs to a rail behind them. When all three were secured in a cage, the police officers placed a cloth hood over their heads and shut the van door.

'What's the hood all about?' said Smudge as they felt the van move away.

'I don't know, but if they were the same bunch of bent bastards from the tower block, they would have shot us getting out of the car, it would have been easier to say we pulled the guns on them, case closed, no awkward questions.'

'I guess so. Are you alright, love? ' Smudge said, hearing Amanda crying.

'No, I wish I'd never found the stupid photos and bloody notebook,' she sobbed.

'Don't worry, I promise you this isn't over yet,' said Danny, his voice determined.

'Yeah, have faith. If Danny says he'll sort it, he'll sort it.'

Amanda stopped crying, and the van descended into quiet. The only sound was the drone of the diesel engine and the rumble of tyres. Although time was hard to gauge with the hood over his head, Danny reckoned they had been going around forty minutes before the van stopped. He heard some muffled voices, then the van moved a little way forward and stopped again. The engine died and the rear doors opened. Hands unlocked them and led them awkwardly down the steps before guiding them into a building. The footsteps behind Danny split and echoed off in different directions. The two men on either side of Danny guided him into a room before hustling him roughly into a seat. They uncuffed one hand and pulled his wrists in front of him before fastening them again. Judging by the echo of their boots and the hard grainy surface with a cold metal object between his wrists, they'd handcuffed him to a metal ring bolted into a heavy wooden table in a bare empty room, probably a police interview room.

With nothing else he could do, Danny relaxed. Interrogators liked to remove the senses, like sight and touch, to play with your head. They leave you alone for a long time, to battle with your own thoughts. A fair percentage of the population caved in the second they start the questioning. It wouldn't work on Danny. They trained him to resist this shit. Everyone caves eventually, but with people like Danny, that would involve painful torture and a lot of it. After a long time, the room door opened and several people entered, two with boots. Rubber soles. Police, army perhaps. One with hard shoes. Leather soles. Dress shoes.

The man in charge is here.

There was a deliberate scrape of metal on concrete as someone dragged a chair out before sitting down. A second later, the hood was whisked off his head. He blinked a few times as his eyes adjusted to the intrusion of the harsh strip lighting. As they acclimatised, Simon's face came into focus, sitting relaxed in the chair opposite, his hands crossed in the lap of his expensive suit trousers.

'Well, well, well, Mr Pearson, what a busy couple of

days you've been having,' he said in his calm Oxford-educated tone, a hint of smugness at having the upper hand creeping into his voice.

'Cut the crap, Simon. Let me out of here,' Danny said, his body tensing as his face hardened, his eyes focused unwaveringly on Simon's.

'My, my, you are a tetchy one. Let me see, let you out of here to do what exactly?' Simon said, still calm, to the point of sounding slightly disinterested.

'I need to make sure Chaz and Fergus are safe, and I need to find who's trying to kill me.'

'Very commendable, dear boy, and I was intent on letting you sort your little problem on your own. That is, until you started turning the capital into a war zone,' Simon said, casually brushing a crease out of his suit trousers.

'What do you want?' Danny said, tired of Simon's games.

'The question is, what do you want, Mr Pearson?'

Danny didn't move for a long time, his mind spinning over various scenarios, none of which worked without Simon's help. He kept up the intense stare until he finally saw the faintest hint of fear in Simon's eyes. He immediately hid it, but Danny saw it all the same.

'I want to make sure Chaz and Fergus are safe, Darren and Amanda are released, and I want to find the Wolf and kill him.'

'Mmm, quite a list for a man facing ten years for firearms offences and a further fifteen for the murder of Anton Kasovich and his men.'

'They were dead when we got there.'

'Well good luck convincing a jury of that one,' Simon said with a smug smile.

'Stop playing fucking games, Simon. What do you want?' Danny said, his patience wearing thin.

'Very well. I help you, but you will do things my way Mr Pearson. It also means you will owe my. Are we in agreement?'

A few more tense seconds went by until Danny finally relinquished and nodded his agreement.

'Excellent, would you mind?' Simon said with a smile, gesturing to Danny's handcuffs.

A man stepped in from behind and unlocked Danny's cuffs, before he and another guy stepped out of the room. Plain clothes, black combat style army boots showing from under their jeans, hard men, military or ex-military, a shoulder-holstered Glock under each arm.

'Do come through, dear boy,' said Simon, gesturing towards the door.

28

Arthur sat in the back of his Bentley in the far corner of a multi-storey car park. The engine was running, keeping the interior a comfortable twenty-four degrees against the freezing early morning air outside. His phone buzzed with a message from Detective Inspector Grant Peeler while he waited.

"Armed response officers attended St Thomas Hospital earlier tonight. A white male with a gunshot wound matching Fergus McKinsey's description was admitted, brought in by a white male answering Charles Leman's description. McKinsey is in intensive care and Leman is in custody at New Scotland Yard. What do you want me to do?"

Arthur pondered the question for a moment before answering.

"It would be a shame if Mr Leman had an accident while in custody. Don't worry about Mr McKinsey. I'll have someone visit him to see how he's doing."

He pressed send just as approaching headlights cast shadows off the concrete pillars. A freshly stolen Audi Q7 came up the approach ramp onto his floor and drove slowly in his direction. It pulled alongside, driving front end in to the space next to Arthur's Bentley which faced nose out. The driver's window lowered as Arthur lowered his rear passenger window. Luka's battle hardened face looked back at him.

'You have it?' Arthur said.

Luka clicked his fingers to a man in the back, he passed him Amanda's bag from the factory. Luka handed it across, waiting silently while Arthur looked at the photos and notebook inside.

'Very good. You managed to get one of them, Fergus McKinsey. He's in the intensive care ward at St Thomas Hospital. I thought you might want to pay him a visit.' Arthur said, his breath visible in the cold air as he looked back at Luka.

Luka responded with a single nod, his eyes still locked with Arthurs, only disappearing when the blacked-out window slid smoothly in front of him, the car immediately reversed out and drove away.

'It's been a long night. Home please, Roger,' Arthur said, sliding his window up against the cold.

'Very good, sir.'

The car moved away with barely a sound. As it rolled down the ramp towards the exit, Arthur made one final call for the night.

'We have Mr Wallace's photos and notebook, Vincent.'

'Good, destroy them. What about Anton and the others?' Vincent fired back quickly.

'Luka has taken care of Anton and we have two of Pearson's men where we can take care of them.'

'Then take care of them, and find the others. Even without the notebook and photos, they could still make trouble for us. If any of them recognise me when I'm Foreign Secretary, awkward questions could be asked. Neither of us can afford the press or anyone else digging too deeply into our affairs,' Vincent said, the pressure of the last few days starting to show in his voice.

'Calm yourself, Vincent, I'll take care of it,' said Arthur, composed as ever.

'Call me when you have news, any time, day or night.'

'Yes Vincent,' Arthur said, hanging up and letting out a tired sigh.

Vincent's paranoid outburst might seem extreme, but he was right about one thing: neither of them could afford people poking into their business affairs.

29

'You might recognise the place. It's had a few changes since you were last here. The interrogation cells, for instance, and...' Simon opened a door and gestured for Danny to enter a high-tech command centre. Men worked at desks with multiple screens. At the far end, a six screen video wall played varying recordings, one of Scott's BMW XB7 skidding to a halt outside St Thomas Hospital, and Danny getting out to help Fergus before Chaz carried him into the A&E department. The others had multiple Wimbledon traffic camera shots of Diggsy's Renault 5 Turbo being chased by Luka's Mercedes G-Class 4x4.

Although fitted out all high-tech and modern, Danny recognised the place as the house in Muswell Hill that he, Paul Greenwood and Edward Jenkins had used to track down a terrorist called Marcus Tenby.

'Where's Smudge and Amanda?' Danny said, shooting Simon a threatening look.

'In the kitchen having a beverage, dear boy, we've got a fantastic little machine that does lattes, cappuccinos and espressos. We even have a little gadget that puts a heart on top when you dust it with cocoa powder. Would you like one?' Simon said dryly.

'What about Chaz and Fergus?' Danny said, ignoring Simon's offer.

'They're safe,' came the familiar voice of Edward Jenkins from behind him.

'Where are they?'

'Fergus is in intensive care at St Thomas'. He's stable. Charles is in a holding cell at New Scotland Yard,' said Edward, gesturing toward a small conference table for them to sit down.

'Get Chaz out or the deal's off,' Danny said, shooting Simon a look.

'You really are an angry fellow. Sit down, Mr Pearson. There are more pieces on this chess board than you are aware of.'

They all sat down. Simon turned to the operative at the computer desk closest to him.

'Whiskins, would you mind getting me a latte? Edward? Mr Pearson?'

'Same, one sugar,' Edward replied.

'Coffee, white, one sugar,' Danny relinquished. He had the feeling he was going to need the caffeine.

'Yes guv,' Whiskins said, heading out the door.

'Ok, I'll bring you up to speed,' said Edward, opening a folder and sliding the QC23 order that Hake sent Police Chief Ryan McGillan from his office. 'The reason

we're here at the safe house is because we have a leak in
MI5. Someone sent an official order to keep out of the
area the night they attacked you and the others. It was
sent to Police Chief Ryan McGillan from my office.'

They all paused as Whiskins brought the drinks.

'Where are David Wallace's notebook and the photos
of the Wolf?' Edward continued.

'Gone. They were at an old factory we were using as a
base. They ambushed us when we returned from Anton
Kasovich's. That's when Fergus got shot.'

'What a shame,' Simon said.

'That's not all. You've got dirty cops in play as well.
We ran into them when we picked up Amanda at a flat
in Paddington. A tower block. Er, Dorchester Place. 25
Dorchester Place. Two guys in police tactical vests and
four more in suits, all armed. Smudge broke the nose of
one of them as they stepped out of the lift.'

'Sorry, did you say Smudge broke his nose?' Edward
said, looking up from his folder.

'Yeah, they came out of the lift and went for their
guns and Smudge cracked one of them on the nose with
the butt of his rifle.'

Edward got up quickly from his seat and moved to
one of the agents nearby. 'Harrison, pull up the SIS
building's vehicle register for the last three days. Find
out which vehicle Peter Utting or Barry Hake signed
out.'

'On it, guv.'

'When you find them, get hold of the boys in
ComTrack and find out every movement they made.'

'Yes guv.'

'Edward?' Simon said.

'Barry Hake took Peter Utting to hospital earlier with a broken nose, some story about him falling down the stairs. We had all the pool cars fitted with GPS trackers last month for insurance purposes. The only people who know about it are myself, the motor pool mechanics, and the guys in admin.'

'Good, let's go and get them. Give me half an hour in one of your interrogation cells. I'll make them talk,' Danny said, his face darkening, frustration, tiredness and anger at Fergus being shot clouding his judgement.

'Now, now, Mr Pearson, we'll deal with Mr Hake and Mr Utting in good time. Why don't you tell us about Mr Wallace's notebook and photos, then get some sleep. There are some cot beds upstairs. You need to rest,' said Simon.

'What about Fergus and Chaz?'

'I have men looking out for Fergus at the hospital. You can see him tomorrow, and Mr Leman will be quite safe in Scotland Yard's holding cell until the morning,' Simon replied.

Danny didn't say anything for a while, his tired brain trying to run through the best course of action but failing.

'Ok,' he finally said, conceding to the fact that if he didn't lie down, he'd probably fall down.

He told Simon and Edward about the photo of the old C-27 Spartan cargo plane landing. The truck with armed Afghan Taliban soldiers arriving to meet it, and the photo of the Wolf and the Taliban spotting David Wallace in his hiding place just before they shot him. Remembering the notebook, Danny told them about the mention of HELP International Humanitarian Aid Group and Wallace's last words, fin or Vin smeared in blood. When he finished, Edward took him through to Smudge and Amanda in the kitchen before showing them to various rooms upstairs set out with army cot beds and clean linen. Danny stripped, turned off the light, and climbed into his cot. He was asleep before the bulb had gone cold.

30

Yesterday's snow had frozen solid in the early morning sub-zero temperatures. The car slipped and crunched along until it found a grip on the freshly gritted New Scotland Yard parking bay. DI Peeler and Detective Billings stepped out and tapped their pass keys on the pad by the door to enter the building. It was still early, getting towards the end of the night shift, but before the bulk of the staff arrived for the busy day ahead. They moved casually through the labyrinth of corridors, ending up outside the comms room. Peeler looked through the glass in the locked door while texting a message. A few seconds later, a chubby, middle-aged, balding man looked up at him from one of the many computer desks. He slipped off his headset as he got up and moved their way, his eyes flicking nervously around the room.

'Jesus, he looks like a school kid who's just had his hand caught in the cookie jar,' said Peeler as the guy slid out of the room.

'H-have you got it?' the little man said, still looking around.

'Stop looking like you've just robbed a bank,' Peeler said, giving him a slap on the side of the head.

'Sorry, Grant, have you got it?'

Peeler reached into his jacket pocket and drew out an envelope full of money. 'You know what you've got to do, Neville?' he said, watching Neville's greedy eyes locking onto the envelope.

'Y-yes, turn off the cameras to the custody suite.'

'Good, and Neville?'

'Yes.'

'Screw this up and that problem with the underage schoolgirl is going to come back to haunt you,' Peeler said, looking Neville in the eyes while holding on tightly to the other end of the envelope as he tried to take it from him.

'I w-won't, Grant, trust me, I'll do it,'

'Good, go on then, jog on,' Peeler said, releasing the envelope.

Neville quickly put it in his pocket and slid back into the command centre. Peeler and Billings watched him go to the far side of the room and enter the comms room, where the building's CCTV equipment was housed.

'God, look at him. He's fucking useless,' said Billings, moving away from the glass.

'Yeah, but unless you've got access to the comms room, he's all we've got. Come on,' said Peeler, heading towards the custody suite.

They stopped short of the door and waited a couple of minutes until the red light went off the camera above the door.

'That's it. Give me a minute to distract the custody sergeant,' said Billings, moving off and entering the custody suite.

He approached the custody sergeant behind the desk with a smile.

'Detective Billings, what brings you here this early in the morning?'

'Hi Donald. There's been a cock-up with the paperwork for Elizabeth Morello. The Chief's doing his nut. I need the arrest sheet and custody records.'

'Is it not on the system?'

'Nah, I reckon some arsehole's hit the delete button by mistake. I need copies of the original.'

'Ok, come on then, I'll print some off,' Donald said, letting Billings behind the desk and into the office behind the custody desk.

Watching them disappear out of sight, Peeler slipped in and darted behind the desk. He looked at Donald's computer and saw an unknown male in cell three, arrested at St Thomas' Hospital, suspected firearms offences. Peeler exited and headed for the cells. He pulled a hypodermic syringe out of his pocket as he walked down the grey corridor to the cell door, filled with enough heroin to overdose an elephant. Quietly lowering the inspection hatch, Peeler looked in side the cell. He could see the shape of Chaz asleep on the hard plastic shelf that acted as a seat or bed. A police issue blanket covered him as he slept. Without moving his eyes off the target, Peeler unlocked the door and pulled it open. Chaz didn't stir as Peeler moved swiftly inside. Walking over on his toes, Peeler stood looking down at the shape under the blanket. He lent down and stabbed the hypodermic needle into Chaz's backside, pushing the plunger down and stood back. Nothing happened, no murmurs, no jerks, no sound. Peeler grabbed the blanket and pulled it back to uncover a training dummy. Anger, confusion and fear hit Peeler all at once. He backed away, turning to leave as fast as he could. A smartly suited man stood in his way.

'I think he's already dead,' Simon said with a cheerful smile.

'I heard a noise and came to check on the prisoner. Who the hell are you?' Peeler said, instantly trying to bluff his way out and leave.

'Of course you did, dear boy. If you don't mind,' Simon said, stepping out of the doorway to reveal four hard-looking men in plain clothes behind him.

Stunned, with his mind racing, Peeler followed Simon out of the cell to see Billings and Neville being led away in handcuffs at the other end of the corridor by more men in plain clothes.

'Who the hell are you, and what am I being charged with?' Peeler protested.

'These gentlemen are Secret Intelligence Service, and you are?' Simon turned to ask him, his voice still upbeat.

'You didn't answer my question. Who are you and

what am I being charged with?'

'No, I didn't, did I?' Simon replied with a smile. 'Gentlemen,' he said, turning to the agents who closed in on either side of Peeler, moving his hands behind his back to handcuff him.

They led Peeler away, leaving Simon in the corridor. He turned to the cell opposite number three and opened the door. Chaz's head looked up from where he was sitting.

'Mr Leman, would you care to join us?' Simon said.

31

Danny awoke with a start, memory flashes of helping
Fergus out of the car, his side all soaked in blood,
replaying in his head in glorious cinematic clarity. He sat
up and took a few deep breaths to chase the images
away. Blinking around the room to focus, he was
surprised to see his old army kitbag from the factory
sitting beside his blood-soaked clothes on the floor from
yesterday. He got up and opened the bag, pulling out
some creased but clean clothes, even more surprised to
see his two bundles of cash still inside. After dressing, he
picked the blood-soiled clothes off the floor and bundled
them into a plastic bag. A cream coloured piece of card
fluttered to the ground as he did so. Bending down to
pick it up, he realised it was the Lansdowne Club
business card with 11AM and the phone number written
on the back. He turned it over in his fingers before
putting it in his back pocket and heading downstairs,
pleased to see Smudge and Amanda sitting around the

kitchen table, tucking into croissants and pastries out of a bag from a local bakery.

'Morning, boss,' Smudge said, turning the bag towards Danny.

'Thanks, mate. Are you alright, Amanda?'

'Better for some sleep. Do you know how your friend Fergus is?'

'That's the next port of call after a coffee and some more of these,' Danny said, grabbing a Danish pastry and heading for the coffee machine.

Refuelled, the three of them went through to the control room. It was empty apart from Harrison and another operative busy tapping away at a keyboard.

'Morning, guys. You sleep well?' Harrison said, getting up to greet them.

'Good thanks. No Simon this morning?'

'No, just me and the new boy, Simon and the rest of the team went out early this morning. They'll be back soon. I've got something for you over here,' Harrison said, smiling over to Whiskins, tapping away on a PC terminal in the corner of the room.

Harrison got up and gestured them over to the conference table. He picked up two leather wallets and pass cards, handing them to Danny and Smudge. When Danny opened it, an MI5 Agent Pearson ID looked back at him.

'Cards to get in and out of here and temporary MI5 ID to use until the present situation is resolved,' Harrison said, noticing the frown on Danny's face. 'I've got these for you as well. That one's yours, Mr Pearson, and this one is yours, Mr Smith,' Harrison continued, handing a mobile phone to each of them.

'Danny, call me Danny,' Danny said to Harrison.

'Yeah and call me Smudge. Everyone does.'

'Me and Smudge are going to see Fergus,' Danny said, telling, not asking.

'Er, ok, fine. There's a Range Rover out front. You can take that. There are two SCO19 armed officers on watch at the hospital, Davis and Barns. I'll inform them you're on your way,' said Harrison, fetching the logbook to sign the car out while Danny and Smudge rolled their eyes behind his back.

'What do I do?' said Amanda, looking a bit lost.

'Ah, I'd like you to go through everything you can remember about your father's notebook and the photos. I've got a Photofit artist coming in to do a profile of the Wolf from what you remember.'

'Ok.'

'You stay here with Harrison. Smudge and I will check on Fergus and then we'll be back,' Danny said, smiling at Amanda before signing for the car.

He took the keys off Harrison and left with Smudge. As they drove out the gate, Harrison looked at the logbook before closing and putting it back in on the shelf. 'Mmm, very amusing,' he muttered at Danny's Mickey Mouse and Smudge's Daffy Duck signatures. 'Ok, Miss Wallace, shall we grab a coffee before we start?'

32

'What's that?' Smudge asked, glancing across from the driving seat at Danny, looking at the Lansdowne Club business card again.

'It's a business card with a phone number and 11Am written on the back. I found it by Anton Kasovich's body.'

'Why didn't you give it to the suits?'

'I don't know. I thought we might check it out for ourselves after we've seen Fergus,' Danny said, opening the MI5 ID with a smile.

'Roger that,' Smudge replied as they passed Big Ben to cross Westminster Bridge with St Thomas visible on the other side of the river.

They turned into the hospital and drove down the ramp to the underground car park, circling around the rows, unable to find an empty parking space.

'Fuck it,' Smudge eventually said, pulling the car into the emergency vehicle drop off bay next to the entrance.

They both got out, locked the car and headed towards the automatic doors. A flustered-looking hospital security guy headed in their direction.

'Here he comes, mini Hitler. Can I?' Smudge said, looking at Danny.

'Knock yourself out, mate.'

'Oi, you can't leave your car there,' the security officer shouted gruffly.

'Excuse me, sir, I'm Agent Smith and this is Agent Pearson. And you are?' Smudge said, his face serious as he shoved his MI5 ID in the man's face.

'Oh, er, well, Terry, Terry Dicks, sir,.' Terry said, the ID stopping him in his tracks.

'Well, Dick, we're here on official business. We have a cobra level five alert.'

'It's Dicks, a cobra what?'

'Cobra level five, Dick. Time is of the essence. Now I need you to look after our car until the rest of our team arrives. When they do, send them up to us, ok?' Smudge continued, his face deadpan as he looked at his watch and jerked his head to Danny, indicating time to go.

'Er, ok. Yes, of course.'

'Good man, I'm counting on you, Dick,' Smudge shouted over his shoulder as they entered the hospital.

'It's Dicks,' Terry grumbled.

'I'm bloody well keeping this when it's all over,' Smudge chuckled as they approached the woman on the reception desk.

'Good morning, we're looking for Fergus McKinsey. He was brought in with a gunshot wound last night?'

Danny said with a smile while flashing his MI5 ID.

'Yes, of course, er…' she replied, looking at his ID

'Agent Pearson.'

'Let me see, yes, he's been moved off the high dependency ward to a room on the Albert ward. It's in the North Wing on the tenth floor.'

Danny thanked her and the two of them followed the signs for the North Wing, with Smudge pressing the lift call button while Danny headed for the stairs.

'Really? Come on, mate, it's the tenth floor,' Smudge said.

'Ok, ok,' Danny said, reluctantly getting into the lift.

'You still got an aversion to lifts then?' Smudge said as Danny stood rigid on the ride up.

'No, I've just got an aversion to being trapped in a kill box with no way out,' he replied through gritted teeth.

'Well nobody's going to shoot us in here, are they?'

'The last time someone said that to me, I was the only one to make it out alive,' Danny said grimly, walking onto the tenth floor.

They pushed their way through the heavy fire doors into the Albert ward. One of the armed SCO19 officers sat by reception.

'Which one are you, Davis or Barns?' Danny said, flashing him his ID.

'Barns. They said you were on your way. He's in the last room on the left, down there. Davis is outside.'

'Cheers.'

They walked down the corridor with nurses and doctors busily going about their duties, flashing their IDs at Davis before entering the room. Fergus lay still in bed. He moved his head slowly in their direction, no reaction on his blank face.

'You alright, Ferg?' Danny said, moving to the bedside.

'I'm not going to make it mate, tell Gaynor and the kids—' he paused to cough weakly. 'Tell them, tell them, they drive me mad and I never liked them anyway.'

'Ferg, you're a fucking idiot,' said Smudge, shaking his head.

'Fair comment. You alright, boys?' he said, cracking a big grin.

'Yeah, we're good. What's the verdict then?' Danny said, pointing to Fergus's bandaged torso.

'The bullet missed any vitals. It hurts like hell when I move, but I should be right as rain in a few weeks.'

'Good. For a minute there, I thought we were going to lose you, mate.'

'Nah, I'm indestructible, me. Saying that, I'm bloody parched. You couldn't fill that water jug up for us, mate? There's a drinks fountain in the corridor.'

'Yeah, no problem,' Danny said, picking up the plastic jug and heading for the corridor.

33

After checking through the slim glass panel that the coast was clear, Luka pushed the door leading from the stairs opposite the lifts open, his right-hand man Goran following closely behind him. They moved towards the Albert ward, pushing the door open before heading casually towards the reception desk, their hands deep in their jacket pockets, neither of them paying any attention to Barns as he gave them a customary look up and down. When they got within a few feet, Luka moved like lightning. His hand shot out of his jacket pocket, grabbing the barrel of Barns's MP5 submachine gun, pushing it forward to trap it tightly across Barns's chest while pulling his father's ornate hunting knife out with the other hand. He punched it deep into Barns's neck before ripping it to one side, its ultra sharp blade slicing through the windpipe. In the same moment, Goran pulled a silenced Beretta from his jacket. The nurse on reception looking up at him, too shocked to move, as he smiled at her before putting a bullet in her forehead. Looking around, Luka dragged Barns, gurgling his last breath, into a curtained cubicle, closely followed by Goran dragging the dead nurse under her arms. They put them on the bed and closed the curtain behind them. Luka slid the knife back into its sheath and drew his silenced Beretta from a shoulder holster. With his gun rock steady on the corridor and Goran's on the entrance to the ward, the two of them stood motionless.

'Barns?' came a voice from somewhere down the corridor and Fergus's room.

***

Danny came out of Fergus's room. He watched Davis moving down the corridor towards reception as he filled the water jug. Something about his body language was on edge, like he was moving cautiously to investigate something.

***

Davis glanced around at the reception area to find it empty. He moved to the entrance doors and pushed them open enough to look out at the corridor outside the ward. No sign of Barns.

'Come in, Barns, do you copy?' he said over his radio, turning at the click of Barns's radio receiving his call from behind a cubicle curtain.

He centred the MP5 submachine gun on the curtain and moved cautiously towards it, the sight of blood dripping onto the vinyl floor underneath the blue material causing his heart to pound as he reached for the curtain. A thud and clang behind him made him jump and spin around, his finger trembling over the trigger, relaxing a fraction at the sight of a porter wheeling a hospital bed through the doors to the ward. He looked at Davis with bored disinterest before pushing the bed into a side room. A cold sweat trickled down Davis's face as he turned, grabbed the curtain and pulled it to one side. He recoiled at the sight of Barns and the dead nurse, their eyes wide open, locked in the terror of their last few seconds.

Davis spun in panic to cover the reception with his gun. It was empty and so quiet you could hear a pin drop. As his eyes fell on the pool of blood on the floor, he froze at the sight of boots under the curtain to his left, his mind clinging to a futile hope that he'd be alright even though he knew he was screwed. Before he could move his gun in their direction, the curtain jerked as bullets from Luka's silenced gun punched little puffs of fabric out on their way to pummeling Davis's torso. As his body hit the floor, Luka and Goran walked out of the curtained cubicle on the left and closed the curtains to the carnage behind them. They moved past the reception desk and darted their heads into the corridor leading to Fergus's room. It was empty. Luka moved on ahead as Goran walked behind him, covering the rear. They positioned themselves on either side of the door. Goran reached across to push it open as Luka swung in, his gun rock steady at the curtain pulled around Fergus's bed. He pulled the trigger, letting off a series of metallic pings, putting two where centre mass should be and two towards the head. Entering the room, Goran ripped the curtain back, only to see a punctured empty mattress and pillow.

'He was just here,' Luka said, placing his hand on the warm bed.

They both rushed back to the corridor just in time to see the back of Danny disappearing out of the ward doors towards the lift and stairs. Luka let off a couple of shots, thumping into the heavy fire door as it closed. With guns up and ready, they ran after him, looking at each other when the fire alarm sounded before they reached the exit. They cautiously opened the doors to see an empty corridor beyond, the light from the open lift ahead of them shining across the vinyl floor.

'He's in the lift,' Luka shouted, both men running forward, swinging their weapons into the empty space inside the lift.

In the second of confusion that followed, Danny burst out of the door to the stairs opposite the lift. Swinging a crutch he'd found in a store cupboard with all his might, he made contact with the side of Luka's head, knocking him to the floor, dazed. Keeping momentum moving, Danny grabbed Goran's gun and shoulder barged him as he turned away from the empty lift, sending Goran and himself flying inside, slamming into its stainless steel back with a boom, the lift door sliding shut behind them. As the gun clattered to the floor, Goran punched Danny hard in the side, separating them to either side of the lift.

The two men immediately took up a fighting stance,

eyes sharp and focused on each other, both men launching into a mixed martial arts form of fighting taught to Special Forces the world over. Ignoring the pain, Danny punched, kicked, and used knees and elbows as Goran did the same. Both men booming off the stainless steel sides of the lift when successful blows found their target, causing the lift to shake and screech as it descended towards ground floor. Bouncing off the side, Danny planted his foot on the shiny surface and propelled himself forward, head-butting Goran squarely on the bridge of his nose. As the cartilage gave way and Goran's eyes glazed and watered, Danny took full advantage. He launched a blistering combination of blows to the body, finishing in a full body weight kick to the balls, sending Goran to the floor as they hit the ground floor. The lift doors pinged open to a sea of armed police pointing guns in Danny's face.

'Whoa, fellas, MI5,' Danny said, holding his hands up while trying to get his breath back. 'There's another one up on ten.'

***

Up on the Albert ward, Smudge opened the store cupboard door opposite Fergus's room and helped his friend across the corridor and back into bed.

'Argh, fuck, that hurts.'

'Stop whining, you tart. It'd hurt a lot more if we hadn't moved you.'

'Yeah, thanks, Smudge mate, I owe you one,' Fergus said, breathing heavily.

'Damn right you do. Just wait until you get better. I'm going to milk this one until it turns to cheese,' Smudge replied with a big grin.

'Oh Christ, I've changed my mind. Get them back in here. They can shoot me now.'

Smudge left Fergus to look out into the corridor. Armed police poured into the ward. Despite locking the building down, there was no sign of Luka.

34

Edward entered the floor to his department in the SIS building. Outwardly, he was calm and said his usual good mornings as he walked. He paused to say good morning to Lorraine before turning to Hake and Utting sitting opposite.

'How the nose, Peter? I heard you took a tumble,' he said with a smile.

'Yeah, my fault, wasn't looking where I was going, hurts like hell but they managed to reset it,' Utting replied, looking up at Edward with two purplish black eyes and a taped-up nose.

'You should be more careful. Have you two looked into the radical group in Greenwich yet?'

'Yes boss, turned out to be nothing. The report's in the system,' said Hake.

'Ok, thank you.'

Edward continued to his office and closed the door. Within a few minutes, he'd pulled up Hake and Utting's schedules and reports for the last few days. Dragging them to a screen on his left, he opened up the ComTrack vehicle tracker report from Harrison. The two didn't match. The GPS tracker put their vehicle at Danny's and then Smudge's house the night of the attack. Further down the list it showed them at 25 Dorchester Place, Paddington, and lastly near Anton Kasovich's house in Wimbledon the night Danny and Smudge were chased. Edward sat back in his chair, a frown appearing on his forehead. He looked through the glass wall across the office at Hake and Utting on the far side. After a minute or two, he picked his phone up and pressed the number for Thomas Trent.

'Hello.'

'Tom, I've got a job for you.'

'Yes boss, what do you need?' Tom said without hesitation.

'I need surveillance on a couple of targets. The works, cameras, phone taps et cetera. Off the books.'

'Off the books? Who's the targets?'

'Two of my own. I need to keep it quiet until I know how far this goes.'

'That's ok, I'll only use my own guys.'

'Thank you, Tom. I'll send you their personnel files now. Report to me, only me, ok?' Edward said, stressing the point.

'Yes boss.'

After pulling the files and sending them to Tom, Edward called Harrison at the house in Muswell Hill.

'Yep.'

'Barry Hake and Peter Utting are our men. I've decided not to pull them. I'm putting them under surveillance to see if they lead us to the source.'

'I thought as much when I saw the locations on the ComTrack report. Ok, I'll let Simon know.'

'Is he there?'

'No, he's up St Thomas' Hospital. A two man hit team tried to finish Fergus McKinsey off. They would have succeeded as well if Mr Pearson hadn't been there.'

'Was anyone hurt?'

'They killed two of SCO19's men and a nurse. One got away, Mr Pearson got the other one out, knocked him clean out. We'll have him back here for questioning as soon as the boss puts a cap on the media and sorts out all the red tape.'

'Ok, I'll be over later. In the meantime, can you run a full financial on Hake and Utting? Whoever they're working for, they must have been paid for it. Let's follow the money and see where it leads.'

'Right, I'll get on it.'

'Thanks, Harrison,' Edward said, hanging up.

He sat back and looked out across the office at Hake and Utting as they shared a joke and laughed with someone on their way out of the office.

Laugh it up, you pieces of shit. I'm coming for you.

35

Danny had to hand it to Simon. Within two hours of arriving, he'd contained the whole situation. Without a crease in his suit or a hair out of place, the government man had Fergus in an ambulance off to a secure private hospital where he'd be safe, and the bodies of the SCO19 officers and the nurse had been removed, along with any trace of what had happened. A few more calls and the press had the name and photos of some radical extremist, with the cover story of a machete attack. Before they knew it, the police and press had dispersed, and they were all downstairs by the cars in the underground car park.

'You and Trevor take the prisoner back to the house and put him in an interview room. I'll be along shortly,' Simon said to the men in a transport van with Goran handcuffed in the back. 'Let's go back to the house,' he continued, turning to Danny and Smudge.

'In a bit. I just want to check something out first,'

Danny said, heading for the Range Rover.

'Anything you care to share?' Simon called after him.

'Nope,' Danny growled back.

Smudge shrugged at Simon and followed Danny. A little smile curled on Simon's face before he turned and got in the back of his car.

'Back to Muswell Hill please, Michael.'

'Yes sir,' Michael said, pulling smoothly away.

***

Trevor turned and banged the metal grill that separated the van's cab from the caged transport cells in the rear. 'Shut up in there,' he shouted at Goran's Serbian rantings.

'What's he going on about?' said Phil, driving.

'How the hell do I know? I don't speak Serbian, do I,' said Trevor, shaking his head at some idiot in an Audi Q7 undertaking them in the bus lane.

'I said, when I get out of here, I'm going to kill you,' Goran growled back in broken English.

'Yeah, yeah, sweetheart, you ain't going nowhere,' Trevor said, turning to blow Goran a kiss.

He turned back just in time to see the Audi Q7 cut in front of them from the bus lane and slam the brakes on.

'Fuck!' shouted Phil, jumping on the brakes, stopping just short of the Audi.

The rear doors shot open. Luka and one of his men spun out from either side with automatic rifles.

'Get us out of here,' Trevor shouted, pulling his Glock out of his shoulder holster. A burst of automatic fire punched through the windscreen and through Trevor before he had a chance to use it.

Phil hit the gas and rammed the back of the Audi, making the men jump away from the car. He threw the van in reverse and floored it, swerving past the car behind them to accelerate backwards down the bus lane.

'Hang in there,' he shouted to Trevor, wheezing and coughing up blood beside him.

Phil spun the van into a side road, grinding the gears into first before heading back the way they came. Looking in the rearview mirror, he saw the powerful Audi spin around and accelerate towards him, its bonnet lifting with every gear change as its 4.2 litre V8 engine powered the car after him.

Phil gunned the sluggish diesel engine for all it was worth, its turbo blowing out black smoke as he clung on to some hope he could get away from Luka. They were up behind him in no time, Luka sliding his torso out of the passenger window while aiming his rifle. He fired a burst at the van's rear tyres. The bullets ripped through the rubber, shredding and deflating them in seconds, causing the van to snake along the road. Undeterred, Phil still kept his foot on the gas. For a second, he thought he was going to make it until the Audi drove into the rear corner of the van, kicking the back end out. With no grip from the flat tyres, it slid sideways, mounting the kerb before slamming into the black iron railings in front of a row of Georgian houses. The back wheels bounced briefly off the floor as the van went from forty to zero in a split second. The front windows blew out with the impact and Phil disappeared from view for a few seconds, hidden by a wall of exploding airbags.

Dazed, Phil looked across at Trevor slumped in the passenger seat, a bloody stain running from his mouth down his front. His eyes stared lifelessly at the floor. The ringing in Phil's ears subsided, and he was aware of the back of the van being opened. Spotting Trevor's gun in the footwell, Phil reached down and grabbed it. As he came back up, the cold metal of a gun barrel pressed into his temple.

'I told you I was going to kill you,' said Goran, his voice calm and menacing.

He pulled the trigger before Phil's panic stricken brain could come up with a response.

'Let's go, come on,' Luka shouted.

He stood behind the Audi, pointing his rifle at the line of stationary cars behind them. Within seconds, Luka and his men were back in the Audi and tearing off into the distance. Scared Londoners sat rooted to the spot, not knowing what to do, mentally ill-equipped to deal with mercenaries brandishing automatic weapons facing them down. The whole incident only took a few minutes from start to finish, but would likely replay in their nightmares for weeks to come.

36

'So where are we going?' Smudge asked Danny.

'I told you earlier, I want to check this Lansdowne Club out,' Danny said, heading for Mayfair.

'Oh right, yeah, and what are we expecting to find there?'

'I don't know, Smudge, but the phone number and 11AM written on the back of the business card must mean something. Perhaps Anton Kasovich was a member, in which case somebody might know who he met there.'

'Sounds reasonable. What kinda club do you think it is?' said Smudge, pulling his phone out to google it.

'It's in Mayfair, Smudge. I don't think it's a lap dancing club, mate,' Danny chuckled.

'I don't know, posh twats like a bird spinning around on a pole as much as the next man,' Smudge said, bringing up the club's website. 'Ah, no, it looks like a club for toffs with a stick up their arse.'

'Not the sort of place a notorious drug dealer in a shell suit would hang out then?' Danny said, glancing across.

'No, mate, looks to me like it's the Oxford and Cambridge boat race lot, politicians and barristers.'

'Well, it's the only clue we've got, so it's worth a shot.'

After giving up on finding a car parking space near the Lansdowne Club, they parked in an NCP underground car park a little way away. If you left your car in the wrong place in Mayfair, it'd be on the back of a lorry and on its way to a police pound before the engine got cold. They walked through Berkeley Square and came to the grand but understated front of the club. If it wasn't for the flag with the emblem of the club and a small plaque outside, you'd never know it was there. They walked through the doors towards the reception desk, instantly getting frowns from the staff at their jeans, trainers and bomber jackets.

'Can I help you, sir?' the smart-suited receptionist said, looking down his nose at Danny.

'Yeah, I'd like to see the manager please,' Danny said, giving a wide smile.

'Do you have an appointment, sir?' the man said, before turning away from them to say, 'Goodbye sir and madam,' to a couple of members leaving, dressed in a blur of Armani, Gucci and Louis Vuitton.

When he turned back, Danny had his MI5 ID in his face. 'The manager, now, please.'

'Of course, Agent Pearson,' he said, trying to hide his annoyance as he picked up the phone. 'Mr Heddon, could you come to reception please? I have some gentlemen from MI5 who would like a word.'

He replaced the receiver and turned back to Danny and Smudge. 'If you'd like to take a seat, he'll be down in a minute.'

They'd barely sat down when an immaculately dressed, skinny, middle-aged man approached them.

'Ralph Heddon, general manager. How can I help you, gentlemen?'

'Agent Pearson and Agent Smith, MI5. We have reason to believe your club might have been targeted by an extremist group located in the capital. I'd like to look at your CCTV and visitor's register for the last few days, if I may. Just in case one of our suspects has managed to enter the club,' Danny said, leaning in towards the manager and speaking quietly.

'I, I don't know, we pride ourselves on our members' privacy. Don't you need a warrant or something?'

'Listen, Ralph, I can leave now and be back in an hour with a hundred officers and a warrant and rip this place apart, or you can let me have a quick look at the CCTV and visitors' register and I'll be on my merry way. Your choice, but make it quick as I have a lot to do today,' Danny said, his look more intense and voice more direct.

Ralph looked from Danny to Smudge, both of them looking at him with unwavering stares.

'Gerald, could you print the visitors' register out for this week please?' he said, turning to the receptionist.

When they had the list, the manager took them down to a small office in the corridors beyond the affluent grandeur of the public areas of the club. A security guard in his fifties sat in a chair with multiple screens in front of him, his back slightly hunched and belly stretching the navy blue jumper from too many hours sitting in the chair, eating snacks to while away the boredom.

'Mr Barret, these gentlemen would like to look through the CCTV. Could you show them whatever they want? I'll leave you in Mr Barret's capable hands,' he said, leaving the room.

'I think that's the first time that old bastard's spoken to me. I didn't know he knew my name. Anyway, what you after, gents?' he said with a grin.

'We'd like to look at all the cameras for the last three days, specifically around 11 a.m.'

'11 a.m, right you are,' he said, tapping on a keyboard to bring up Monday, then scrolling back to 10:45 a.m.

With thirty cameras across the building, it was hard to see the detail on the chequerboard of feeds spread across the three screens in front of them.

'Can you just have the outside, reception and stairs?' Danny said, pointing to the little squares.

'Yep, hang on a sec.'

Barret moved the mouse around and selected the three cameras, pulling one feed into each screen.

'That's great, if you can move it forward.'

Danny and Smudge scanned the cars coming and going and guests as they entered the reception between 10 a.m and midday for the first two days, then got Barret to fast forward to yesterday.

'What are you looking for?' Barret asked.

'A dodgy-looking Albanian drug dealer in a shell suit,' Smudge muttered to himself.

'Er, we're not really sure, a familiar face, someone who shouldn't be there,' Danny said, starting to give up as yesterday's 10 a.m to midday floated past into late afternoon without anyone standing out.

'Well, it was a long shot. Thanks, mate, we'll leave you to——' Danny stopped mid-sentence. A car arriving caught his eye as the feed fast forwarded through yesterday. 'Hang on, back it up, more, keep going, stop there.'

'What are we looking at?' said Smudge, confused.

'The number plate on the Bentley,' Danny said, pointing to the personalised number plate.

'I'll be damned,' Smudge said, looking at the 11AM on the plate.

'Go back, find the guest that got out of that car.'

'Ah, that's easy. That's him, Arthur Montgomery. He's a regular here, mixes with the Members of Parliament a lot.'

'Where's he going?' Danny asked, seeing Arthur disappear from the view of the stair camera.

'The second floor restaurant I imagine,' Barret said, flicking the camera feeds to show a plush restaurant fitted out in tasteful blues and greens.

In the middle was Arthur Montgomery greeting someone at a table. The man had his back to them, his body shape and sandy coloured hair looked familiar to Danny, but he wasn't sure why. As both men sat down, a waiter came over to take their order. The man's head turned to talk to him, giving an insincere million-dollar smile as he did so.

'Freeze it there. That's him,' Danny said, taking a picture of the screen on his phone.

'That's who?' Smudge said, confused.

'The Wolf, that's him, a hundred percent, same hair, same body shape and same smile as the man in David Wallace's picture. Who is that?' Danny said, tapping the screen in front of Barret.

'Sorry, I don't know him. He'll be in the visitors' register as a member, or Mr Montgomery's guest.'

'Thanks, can you fast forward it and see if you can get a better view of him leaving?' Danny said, looking down to see his phone ringing. 'Hello.'

'Ah, Mr Pearson, I'm not sure what you're doing at the Lansdowne Club, but would you mind finishing up and joining us at the house? There's been a development.'

'What kind of development?'

'The bad kind,' Simon said, hanging up.

'Simon wants us back at the house,' Danny said to Smudge.

'How'd he know we were here?'

Danny held the phone up and shook it at Smudge.

'Ah, yeah, figures.'

Barret managed to get a slightly better image of the Wolf as he left the club. Danny and Smudge thanked him and left with the copy of the visitors' register. They trudged back through Berkeley Square to the car park, got back to the car and headed towards the house in Muswell Hill.

37

It was a little after five by the time they got back to the house, but in the depths of an English winter, the sun had already dropped below the horizon, the temperature dropping with it. They moved swiftly to the door, tapping the card Harrison had given them on the pad beside it. The lock buzzed, and they went inside, welcoming the warmth that hit them from within. The control room was alive with people, a hum of multiple conversations all going at once filling the room. Edward spotted them from the far side and weaved his way over.

'Glad you're back. I heard all about the hospital. You both alright?'

'We're fine. What's going on here?' Danny said, nodding towards the activity.

'The prisoner transport got hit on its way over here, two dead and no sign of your friend from the hospital.'

'Shit. These guys are really starting to piss me off,' Danny growled.

'That makes two of us,' Smudge agreed.

'That makes three of us,' came Chaz's voice from behind them.

'Chaz, good to see you, brother. When did you get here?' Danny said, his mood instantly lifted.

'This morning, Simon brought me back after he caught two of the blokes from the tower block shooting, trying to ice me in the cells. They're only bloody detectives in the Met.'

'What? Where are they?' Danny said, his mood instantly doing a one-eighty.

'They've got them in an interview room out back. Hang on, Danny, mate, I know that look,' Chaz said as Danny pushed past him.

'Oh shit,' Smudge said as the two of them and Edward headed after him.

Danny passed through the kitchen on his way to the cells, sliding two knives out of the wooden block on the side as he went, flipping the blades upwards and sliding them up the sleeves of his jacket.

'Has he talked yet?' Danny said to the guard, looking at Peeler through the one-way glass in the observation room beside the cell.

'Not yet. They're both playing the no comment game and demanding a lawyer. Simon's letting them sweat for a while before he goes back in.'

'Which one's that?' Danny said, pointing through the glass.

'That's Detective Inspector Grant Peeler.'

'Thanks, mind if I have a go?' Danny said, already

moving to the interview room door.

'Hey, what? No, the boss said no one's to go in until he gets back. Hey,' the guard yelled, heading after Danny as Chaz, Smudge, and Edward caught up to see the interview room door shut in their faces.

Inside, Danny whipped the empty metal chair opposite Peeler away, jamming it under the handle of the steel lined door. It rattled as the guard outside tried to open it in vain. Turning slowly towards the room, Danny saw the fear in Peeler's eyes as he recognised him from the tower block. He quickly covered it.

'What's this then, eh, you supposed to scare me? Because it ain't working. I'm not saying anything until I see my lawyer,' he said, folding his arms and staring defiantly.

Outside, they gave up trying to push the door open and piled into the observation room to see what was going on.

'Look at the picture,' Danny said, pulling up the picture of Arthur and Vincent from the Lansdowne Club's CCTV and sliding his phone across the wooden table to face Peeler. Unfolding his arms, Peeler picked the phone up and gave it a dismissive look before putting it down and resting his hands flat on the table.

'Never seen them before. Now I want my phone call and my lawyer.'

Quick as lightning, Danny's hand came down, thumping the knife from the kitchen through the bone, muscle and tendons of the back of Peeler's hand before spiking it into the wooden table underneath, leaving

Peeler looking at it in shock and horror.

'You're fucking mad, help, someone help,' he screamed, the nerves in his hand exploding with little electric pulses of excruciating pain with every tiny movement he made.

'Let's try that again. Tell me about you, Anton Kasovich, Arthur Montgomery and this man,' Danny said, sliding the phone forward again and tapping on Vincent's picture.

'Go fuck yourself,' Peeler spat in between heavy breathing against the pain.

Faster than Peeler could blink, Danny thumped the second kitchen knife through the back of Peelers' other hand, pinning him to the table for a second time.

'Argh, no more. I'll tell you, please, I'll tell you.'

'Go on, and don't bullshit me, because I'll know,' Danny said, grabbing the handles of the knives and flexing them from side to side, setting every nerve in Peeler's body on fire.

'Stop, Christ, I'll tell you, just stop,' Peeler blurted, his breathing heavy as sweat trickled down his forehead.

Danny let go of the knives and stood back while Peeler took quick breaths to fight the pain. His face dark and menacing, Danny leant forward, thumping his hands down on the table to get Peeler talking.

'Whoa, whoa, no, ok. I'll tell you. A couple of years ago me and Billings were getting ready to bust Anton Kasovich. Somehow, they got wind of it and ambushed us. We were told we either work for them or they kill us and all our family. They paid money into an offshore account for us. We received orders over the phone from Anton or the man above him, a posh type, no name. He'd change the numbers every few days and text us a new one. He wasn't the man at the top, only the posh guy and Anton knew who that was. I overheard Anton on the phone once. He called him the Wolf. That's all I know. We never met him and I don't know who the men in the picture are.'

Danny dragged the phone back and turned, pulling the chair away from the door to open it.

'I'll fucking have you for this, you fucking psychopath.'

'No, you won't, and you better pray you never see me again, because next time I'll put a bullet in your head,' Danny said over his shoulder, before walking calmly past the others in the observation room back towards the control room.

38

'What the hell was that?' Edward said when he caught up with Danny.

'Listen, I've spent the last three days getting shot at, chased and my best mate's in hospital. You want results, I'm getting results, ok? Now the guy on the left is the Wolf, and the guy on the right is his go between, Arthur Montgomery. They gave the order to Anton Kasovich to kill all of us. When he screwed it up, they paid the same bunch of mercenaries who shot Ferg and ambushed your transport, to kill Kasovich and close the link to them,' Danny said, handing Edward the phone with the picture of Arthur and Vincent on it.

'Are you sure about this?' Edward said with a surprised look on his face.

'One hundred percent. I found this card by Anton Kasovich's body. I thought the 11AM was a meeting time at the club so I checked it out. It's not, it's Arthur Montgomery's personalised number plate. And the other guy matches the image in the pictures David Wallace took of the Wolf, same body shape, same hair, same smile, I'm sure of it.'

'That gentleman there is Vincent Benedict MBE, rumoured to be announced as the Foreign Secretary in the upcoming cabinet shuffle on the eighteenth, and Arthur Montgomery is a renowned government adviser and personal friend to the Prime Minister,' Edward said, raising his eyebrows at Danny.

'I don't give a shit if they're members of the royal fucking family. Let's go get them. I'll make them talk.'

'Much as I admire your enthusiasm, and your penchant for kitchen knives, Mr Pearson, the fact is, other than a tenuous link from the back of a business card and your recollection of a man's face from an old photo taken at a distance, with sunglasses and a baseball cap on, we have no evidence of any wrongdoing by these gentlemen. I'm not saying they are not who we're looking for. I'm just saying these men are extremely well connected. If we put one foot wrong, heads will roll. There are certain people who would delight in tying this department up in red tape for the foreseeable future or closing us down altogether,' said Simon, stepping into the room.

'So we do nothing?' Danny said, shooting him an angry look.

'Now, I didn't say that, did I?' Simon replied, his smile and arrogance annoying Danny even further.

'What then?'

'Much as I can not condone what you did to Mr

Peeler, I can not deny the effectiveness of your interview technique. I imagine if he's given the choice of a deal or an hour alone with yourself, he might be ready to do a deal.'

'And how does that help us?' growled Danny.

'My dear fellow, I fear you're missing the bigger picture. Mr Peeler has a current contact number for the man who gives the orders. If we get Mr Peeler to call that number and report the demise of Charles Leman, while we track the cell and put an observation crew on Mr Montgomery, we then have an undeniable link between the two, and grounds for a full investigation into Mr Montgomery and his associate, Vincent Benedict.'

'Great, I'll sit here with my thumb up my arse while you play detective. Meanwhile, a bunch of mercenaries are trying to kill me and my men.'

'My, my, we are bad tempered today. Now, if you'll allow me to finish, I'll explain how we are going to take care of our little group of mercenaries.'

'Go on.'

'We have two MI5 agents under observation. I believe you met them at the tower block the other day. If we feed them the right information, we can set a trap for our little bunch of paid killers while we build a case on Mr Montgomery and Vincent Benedict. Now, myself and Edward have some organising to do, so if you'll be a good chap and keep out of the way, preferably without injuring anyone else, it would be most appreciated,' Simon finished, turning away towards Edward and dismissing Danny without a second thought as he put the wheels in motion.

'Come on, mate, let's leave them to it,' said Chaz, nodding towards the exit.

'I really fucking hate that bloke,' Danny grumbled on the way out.

***

An hour later, Simon and Edward stood over Peeler.

'You understand this is your one chance to walk out of here, make the call, and you'll be discharged from the force with a clean record,' said Simon.

'And my police pension?' Peeler said, cradling his bandaged hands in his lap.

'Not a chance. Make the call, Mr Peeler, or the deal's off and I'll let Mr Pearson deal with you however he sees fit.'

'Ok, ok, I'll make the call,' Peeler quickly answered, nodding frantically in agreement.

'Good,' Simon said, calm as usual.

Harrison looked up from his laptop. He picked up Peeler's mobile and dialled the latest number for Arthur Montgomery.

It rang for an excruciatingly long time before finally being answered.

'Mr Peeler, I've been waiting for your call.'

39

In one of the plush function rooms of The May Fair hotel, Mayfair, Arthur Montgomery sat at a large round table with Vincent Benedict on one side, and the Prime Minister with his wife on the other. The Lord Chancellor and his wife sat opposite. They were enjoying an exquisite three course meal, with fine wines and champagne before the charity auction began. Arthur's mobile buzzed silently in his pocket, not the pocket with his regular phone in, but the one with the phone for other business. He dabbed the corners of his mouth with a napkin before getting up. Straightening his tuxedo, he excused himself, smiling and patting the Prime Minister on the back before heading out of the room towards the area beyond the restrooms.

'Mr Peeler, I've been waiting for your call.'

'Sorry, it's been really hard to get out. The top brass are calling for a full investigation into a prisoner dying of an overdose in one of our cells.'

'So you were successful then?'

'Yes, Charles Leman is dead, and I just heard Fergus McKinsey died of a massive heart attack while being transferred from St Thomas' to a private hospital.'

'Excellent, Mr Peeler. Any news of the others?'

'Not from my end. MI5 has taken over the investigation. You'll have to ask Hake,' Peeler answered, a little nervousness showing in his voice.

'Is everything ok, Mr Peeler?' Arthur said slowly.

'Yes, fine, I just need to keep my head down for a few days until all this blows over.'

'Very well, I'll text you a new contact number in a few days,' Arthur said, hanging up.

He looked around slowly. Guests from the function hall wandered to and from the restrooms. One of the serving staff stood over by the fire exit talking on his phone while he took a five-minute break; nothing struck Arthur as out of the ordinary, so he dialled Hake's number.

'Hello.'

'Mr Hake, I believe the girl and our group of gentlemen are now of MI5's interest?'

'Hang on,' Hake said, pausing the call as he exited the office and got out of earshot of his work colleagues. 'Rumour is Jenkins is looking after them personally. He's moving them out to a safe house in Essex tomorrow. I'll send you the address as soon as I get it.'

'Very good, Mr Hake. This phone will be off shortly. I'll text you a new number in due course,' Arthur said, hanging up.

Walking over to the bin, Arthur pulled the back off the burner phone and removed the battery and sim, snapping the little card before binning them. Holding the phone in both hands, Arthur snapped it in half and tossed it in after the sim and battery. He turned, straightened his jacket and fixed the public smile back on his face, before pushing through the double doors and making his way back to the table.

'Everything ok, Arthur?' Vincent said, leaning in to ask him in a low voice.

'Everything is extremely ok, Vincent. To future plans,' he said, picking up his champagne glass and raising it to Vincent.

Out in the hall by the restrooms, the waiter was back on his phone and walking towards the bin.

'Yes sir, I filmed him while I pretended to be on the phone. Yes sir, I have a good shot of him dumping the phone after the second call. Yes sir, I'm retrieving it now,' he said, ending the call to Simon before taking the lid off the bin and taking the entire contents out in the bin bag. He replaced the lid and moved over to the fire escape, punching the bar to open the door before heading out into the car park and into a waiting car.

'Alright, Brian,' the driver said as he got in.

'Yeah, the boss wants this over at forensics straight away.'

'They got the lot then?'

'Yep, cell provider tracking, a time stamped video of him answering Peeler's call, and calling Hake's number, and we've got the phone with his fingerprints and DNA on it,' Brian said, holding up the bin bag.

'Best we get a move on then.'

40

'You two good with this?' Danny said to Smudge and Chaz.

'What, being the bait to catch a bunch of psycho mercenary killers? Yeah I'm peachy,' said Chaz with a grin.

'Smudge?'

'Yeah, what he said,' Smudge said, winking at Amanda while checking the standard issue Glock handgun they'd been given.

'What about you, Amanda? Are you ok with this? You don't have to be here if you don't want to,' Danny said, turning towards her as she sat at the kitchen table looking lost. Members of Simon's armed tactical response unit wandered past her as they set up locations in the old farmhouse to ambush Luka's mercenaries.

'No, I'm fine. The sooner this is over, the sooner I get my life back,' she replied, managing a smile.

'Good, try to relax. I doubt anything will happen in

daylight,' Danny said, smiling back at her.

'Morning, gentlemen, settling in alright?' came Simon's voice as he entered the farmhouse, shaking the snow off his trench coat.

'Yes sir, we've got two in the barn, two upstairs and two covering the doors front and back. We also have two teams on the road covering the east and west approaches,' said the officer in charge.

'Good man, eyes and ears?'

'Online sir, body cams all online and linked with control, plus four cameras on the house and two in the woods covering the drive and rear of the house.'

'Thank you, Sergeant,' Simon said, shaking his hand before moving over to Danny.

'Everything ok with you, Mr Pearson?'

'Terrific, are your men any good?' Danny said bluntly, sliding the Glock into his tactical vest.

'All highly trained, Mr Pearson. If they take the bait, we'll have them. They won't get past Sergeant Foster and his men.'

'Why not? I could,' Danny said, locking eyes with Simon.

'Have some faith, Mr Pearson. All will be fine. Right, I must be off,' he replied cheerfully, ignoring Danny's comment.

They watched him drive off through the farmhouse's large criss-cross leaded window. The snow blowing off his car roof as he accelerated down the long drive to the main road.

'Anything goes wrong, we watch each other's backs

and protect her,' Danny said, nodding subtly over towards Amanda.

'Roger that,' Smudge and Chaz said together.

Morning moved slowly into afternoon, the clock above the fireplace dragging its heels through each long hour. When the fire started to dwindle, Danny headed out to the woodshed. The woods surrounding the farmhouse were already oppressively dark, the black snow clouds above blocking out the winter's sinking sun. It would be pitch black within the hour. He picked up some logs, noticing a propane gas cylinder by an old rusty barbecue in the corner of the shed. A sound, or maybe a sense made the hairs on the back of Danny's neck stand on end. He dropped the logs, twisting and pulling his Glock all in one smooth movement. The barrel of his gun was in the face of one of the TAC units' faces before they could blink.

'Whoa, stand down, I'm on your side,' the young officer blurted out in panic, the sight of a gun barrel between his eyes rooting him to the spot.

'You come up behind me again, son. You announce yourself, you got it?' Danny said gruffly, his face unemotional as he slipped the gun away and picked up the logs for the fire.

'Yes, sir. Sorry, sir,' he said, scooting off towards the barn in a hurry.

'Some protection they are, Chaz,' Danny said into the inky black shadows down the side of the farmhouse.

'They're just a bit wet behind the ears, mate. I bet he was an A-star student at the academy,' Chaz said, emerging silently out of the darkness to follow Danny towards the farmhouse door.

'How reassuring,' Danny grumbled.

'Cheer up, you miserable bastard. I think you're getting a little cynical in your old age,' Chaz chuckled, making Danny smile.

'Come on, let's get in. It stinks out here. I think your A-star student just shit himself.'

Inside, Smudge was talking to Amanda, warm idle chit-chat to keep her calm and her mind off the horrors of the last few days. He looked relaxed to the untrained eye, but Danny and Chaz knew he was on alert, his eyes only leaving the window to acknowledge them as they entered the room before returning to the darkening view of the drive curling its way through the trees towards the road beyond.

41

'It's coming down heavy again,' said Sergeant Foster's man, sitting in the car by the side of the road on the east approach to the farmhouse.

'The news said it's the worst winter for ten years,' his partner in the passenger seat replied.

'Yeah, and we've got to sit out here in the middle of it on this bullshit detail.'

'Well, the top brass seem to think there's a genuine threat.'

'How many other genuine threats have we been sent on that turned out to be nothing?' the driver said, flicking the wiper on to clear the snow from the windscreen.

'Mmm, fair point, whoa what's that?' he said as a burst of white noise filled his earpiece.

'Hello, hello, Mike One to base, come in base. Great, now the radios down.'

'Give it a minute. If it doesn't come back on, we'll

drive to the house and see what's up,' he said, looking out into the woods from the passenger seat.

The snow reflected what little light there was, giving the foreground a luminescent glow against the inky blackness beyond the tree line. As he continued to look absentmindedly, he blinked in disbelief; a snow covered shrub a few metres from the car unfolded before his eyes.

He managed to say, 'What the fuck?' before Goran lifted a fully automatic silenced Uzi from underneath his snow-camouflaged ghillie suit, emptying the magazine into the two officers in the car. He stepped forward, throwing the empty magazine on the floor before sliding in a fresh one, glancing at the dead officers with little interest before turning away.

'East approach is clear. Come and get me,' he said in Serbian over his throat mic.

'West approach is clear,' came another Serbian voice over the earpiece.

'We are on our way,' Luka responded over the noise of an engine.

A few moments later, a white Ford Transit van appeared around the bend in the road and slid to a stop beside Goran. The side door slid back, and he climbed in beside another man in a camouflage ghillie suit holding a large electronic device on his lap, a wire leading off it through the rubber seal of the rear door to a magnetic antenna on the roof of the van.

'The jammer is working good, yeah?' Goran said.

'Yeah, it'll block out any frequency apart from our

comms for five hundred metres in all directions.'

'Good, let's go,' Goran said, sliding the side door shut.

They drove the hundred yards to where the dirt drive headed into the woods towards the farmhouse. A van that had taken out Sergeant Foster's men covering the west approach arrived at the same time. Luka flashed the other van to turn into the drive ahead of him, both vehicles stopping when they were just out of sight of the road. They got out and joined the ghillie suited passenger as he got out of the other van. Luka walking past him to talk to the driver.

'As soon as we're in position, I'll give you the command. Ok?'

'Ok?'

Luka leant in and looked over the seat to a man in the back. 'Are you all ready?'

'Da,' came the reply.

Stepping back, Luka closed the passenger door and spun his finger in the air. The four men, barely visible in their camouflage suits, fanned out and disappeared into the tree line.

'Comms check. One.'

'Two.'

'Three.'

The sound offs came through until they heard all six men.

'The cloud is clearing, let's get a move on,' Luka said, looking up through the tree canopy at a bright full moon edging its way out from behind thinning snow clouds.

Back at the van, the driver turned it around and

reversed it towards the farmhouse, stopping while it was still out of sight in the trees. The driver hopped out of the cab and went to the rear. Opening the doors wide, he clicked a latch into place to stop them from closing again. He gave a nod to his comrade in the back before climbing back into the driver's seat.

42

'Sarge, you got comms? My earpiece isn't working.'

'Mike One, Mike Two, come in, all units sound off. No, mine's dead too. Check the guys upstairs for me.'

'Yes sir.'

Hearing the conversation, Danny and Chaz were already on their feet and moving to each side of the large criss-cross patterned front window.

'Amanda, let's go and make a cuppa for the lads,' Smudge said, smiling to Amanda, enticing her away from the front of the house. She looked nervously back at Danny and Chaz moving to the windows as she followed Smudge into the kitchen.

'You see anything, Chaz?'

'Nah, you?'

'Not yet.'

'It could just be dodgy comms,' Chaz said, throwing Danny a wishful look.

'No, phone signal's out as well,' Danny replied,

looking up at him from his phone.

'Shit, I hate it when I'm wrong. Hold up, I see movement.'

Sergeant Foster hurried into the room, followed by the young guy Danny had met at the woodshed. They moved to the windows, opening them before kneeling on the floor and taking aim with their MP5 submachine guns. A second later, the shadowy shape of a Transit van came into view, reversing at speed along the driveway, the gearbox whining as it went. They could see the back doors pinned open, but the inky blackness from within giving nothing away as to its contents.

Short bursts of muzzle flash erupted from Sergeant Foster and his man beside them. More came from the bedrooms above and the barn to the left, lighting up the courtyard like fireworks on bonfire night. Sparks pinged off heavy metal plates welded to the inside of the wide open rear doors and something filling the middle of the van. As it reversed closer, the van came within the floodlight sensors, clicking them on to fill the courtyard with light from powerful 500 watt halogen bulbs.

'Get down,' Danny shouted as an M134 Gatling gun mounted between two metal shields appeared inside the van under the bright lights, its six barrels whistling as they started spinning. Tucked in behind metal shields, the operator wore a heavy duty panelled bulletproof vest, his head protected behind a full face bulletproof mask. Only his eyes were visible through small round holes. As Danny and Chaz hit the floor, the M134 let rip with 4000 rounds per minute at Sergeant Foster and the young man beside him, blowing them back into the room along with a million fragments of glass, wood and brick chips, in a deafening sweep of destruction before the operator moved the aim upstairs. A cascade of wood and chips of brick rained down past the glassless living room window like a twinkling waterfall. Seconds later the gunman swung the gun around on its pintle mount, shredding the wooden panelled barn and Foster's men within. Danny and Chaz fast crawled across the floor, picking up the dropped MP5s from Sergeant Foster and the man next to him.

'I've gotta take this fucker out or we're sitting ducks. Give me a minute then draw his fire,' Danny said, fast crawling for the side door to the woodshed.

'What? Draw his fire? How do you suggest I do that?' Chaz shouted over the deafening gunfire.

'I don't know. Tell him one of your jokes. That should do it,' Danny yelled back before sliding out the door.

'Very funny. Why is it always me?' Chaz muttered to himself, crawling along the floor to the far side of the room. 'Smudge, you both ok in there?' Chaz shouted through to the kitchen as he went.

'Yeah, we're both ok,' came Smudge's shout back.

'Check the exit to the rear. I think we're going to be leaving in a hurry.'

'Roger that.'

Outside, Danny darted across to the woodshed. Moving to the back, he grabbed the propane gas cylinder by the old barbecue and shook it. It was nearly full. He moved forward to the stack of logs and peeped around at the van and the gunman, as he let rip at the upstairs and the last of Foster's men. Looking at his watch, Danny counted down to one minute, spinning the valve on the gas cylinder fully open as the last few seconds ticked by. A minute to the second, Chaz fired off a quick burst, the bullets ricocheting off the gunman's bulletproof face mask causing him to flinch backwards. Seeing his moment, Danny charged forward, swinging the heavy cylinder before hurling it as hard as he could at the gunman. It caught him in the chest, knocking him to one side before crashing into the back of the driver's seat. Sliding to a halt, Danny changed direction, his legs powering him back. He dived behind the woodpile and hit the ground just as the gunman got his hands back on the M134 Gatling gun to pull the trigger. Hundreds of rounds blew the logs on the other side of Danny to pieces, before the muzzle flash ignited the growing volume of invisible gas filling the back of the van from the hissing propane cylinder. The fireball blasting the burning gunman out of the rear doors before blowing the windows out of the front of the van, frying the screaming driver as he scrambled unsuccessfully at the driver's door to get out. Crossing back to the side door into the farmhouse, Danny spotted Goran appear near the woods as he threw off his ghillie camouflage, his eyes visible in the glow from the burning van. Catching more movement to Goran's right, Danny got eyes on Luka's men throwing off their camouflage suits. Without hesitation Danny shoulder charged the side door, falling inside as bullets embedded themselves into the heavy oak above his head.

'Here they come. Time to go Chaz,' shouted Danny, heading for the kitchen to join Smudge and Amanda at the back door.

43

'Milica, you and Vesna take the front, me and Goran will circle round back and cut anyone off. Kill everyone, no witnesses, no mistakes,' Luka said over his throat mic.

'Yes boss, no mistakes,' said Milica, moving off cautiously with Vesna towards the front door of the farmhouse.

Luka took point, working around the back of the woodshed to the rear of the house. Inside, Danny dashed into the kitchen and dived under the sink, picking up bottles one by one, reading the label and chucking them behind him until he found some bleach and ammonia-based kitchen cleaner.

'Check the back,' he shouted to Chaz as he emptied the bottles into a large saucepan. 'Smudge, you and Amanda head for the tree line. Then cover us as we come across,' Danny continued, chucking the empty bottles behind him.

'It's clear,' Chaz said, looking out the back.

'Roger that,' Smudge said, taking Amanda's hand and leading her outside. 'Don't worry, love, stick close to me and we'll be alright, but we've gotta keep moving, ok?'

'Ok,' she replied with a nod. Her eyes looked trustingly into his before he led her out into the bitter cold to disappear into the darkness of the trees. Once under cover, Smudge turned and whistled the all clear to Chaz, his head flicking left and right in time with his gun, ready to fire at any hostiles.

'Time to go,' Danny said, putting the gas hob on full and placing the saucepan on top before heading out the back door.

'What's with the domestics?' Chaz said when they reached Smudge in the trees.

'Bleach and ammonia makes chloramine at best, or hydrazine at worst. Either way, you don't wanna be in that kitchen once it starts boiling. Come on, if we head due south through the woods for a couple of miles, we should hit the Chelmsford road.'

'Roger that, boss.'

'Smudge, take point with Amanda. Me and Chaz will hang back and cover the rear.'

'Got ya, come on, the sooner we get going, the sooner we get you safe and warm,' Smudge said, using the moonlight reflecting off the snow in between the trees to pick a route through the trunks and branches.

Just before Smudge was out of sight and earshot, Chaz followed, turning after thirty seconds to go down on one knee, his eye glued to the rifle sight as he scanned past Danny towards the light of the farmhouse in the distance. Danny overtook him to repeat the action, covering Chaz thirty seconds further on.

Back at the farmhouse Milica and Vesna moved swiftly through the rooms, shooting dead the last of Sergeant Foster's men as he hung onto the bannister, trying to get downstairs with bullet wounds to his leg and shoulder. Moving on, they swept into the kitchen, too intent on neutralising any human threat to register the hazy gas filling the air from the bleach and ammonia based cleaner bubbling away on the hob. The instant they took their first breaths, the chloramine gas burned its way down their throats, setting their lungs on fire. At the same time, it hit their eyes, causing them to burn and stream, turning their vision into a blurry haze. Milica, being closer, managed to reach the back door, falling out onto his hands and knees into the cold night air. Luka and Goran approached from the side of the farmhouse to see him vomit violently, trying desperately to suck air into his damaged lungs, before losing consciousness and collapsing facedown in the snow. Goran stepped over him and looked into the gas filled kitchen. Vesna lay on the kitchen floor, barely breathing. Goran let his rifle swing down on the shoulder strap and drew his handgun. Without a word or change of expression, he put two bullets into Vesna before turning and putting one in the back of Milica's head.

'Dead weight,' he said to Luka.

Without bothering to answer, Luka squatted down and followed the footprints in the snow with his eyes as they disappeared into the woods.

'Come, we finish this,' he said, heading off.

Goran holstered his handgun and swung the rifle back up before following Luka into the darkness of the trees.

'Split twenty metres apart. We flank them, then cut them down,' whispered Luka over the throat mic.

'Ok,' Goran replied, moving off to the left before straightening up and moving swiftly through the trees.

A hundred metres on, deep in the trees, Danny and Chaz had stopped relaying and covering to move forward at a fast walk to catch Smudge and Amanda. They stopped now and then, rooted to the spot, barely breathing as they fought the urge to shiver against the cold, while listening for the faintest sound of rustling or twigs breaking that might indicate someone following. When none presented themselves, they moved onwards, reaching the next stop position to turn around and stare into the darkness once more, listening for the sound of anyone approaching.

'There's something not right here. Do you think they'd go through all this trouble not to follow us as we get away?' Danny whispered to Chaz.

'Perhaps they haven't worked out where we went,' said Chaz unconvincingly.

Danny gave him a look that said it all.

'Ok, stupid comment, so where are they then?'

'Where would you be?' Danny said, sinking slowly to the ground to look out to his right.

'I'd go wide and flank us, before cutting us down in a kill box,' Chaz said, sinking to the floor to look out to the left.

Seeing them go down, Smudge put his fingers to his lips to Amanda and indicated down as they both sank to the floor, tucking in behind the tree trunks.

'Ok, where the hell are you?' Chaz whispered.

'Smudge, take Amanda. Go thirty metres forward and let off two short bursts, then take cover,' Danny whispered, handing Smudge the submachine gun.

'Don't you want it?' Smudge asked.

'Nah, too many trees. This calls for close quarters,' Danny said, sliding the Glock handgun out of its holster.

'Agreed. Amanda take this, safety's off. Anyone other than me and Danny comes through those woods, you pull the trigger, ok?' Chaz said, handing his MP5 over and drawing his own handgun.

'Now go Smudge, draw them out and we'll take care of them,' Danny said.

44

It took Smudge and Amanda nearly three minutes to move thirty metres forwards, feeling their way through the tree branches, shrubs and brambles. Danny moved out to the right, ignoring what was behind him. Chaz was covering that. He moved slowly, testing his footing as he went to keep the noise to a minimum, his head always level, looking for the slightest movement. He stooped down and pushed his hands through the snow into the mud beneath, clawing clumps of freezing mud free, smearing his face and clothes before continuing on, invisible in the dark. Two bursts of gunfire filled the air as Smudge reached his mark, shattering the tense silence and causing startled birds to flap and call as they flew away in fright.

There you are.

A small black silhouette moved nimbly from tree to tree at the edge of the woods, stopping behind each one before moving on. The silvery white moonlight reflected off the snow-covered field beyond the woods, showing his outline as he moved toward Smudge's gunfire. Sliding his Glock out of the holster, Danny felt sharp metal. He ran his finger along a deep gouge on the side of the gun, checking it further confirmed his fears. A stray bullet had hit the gun in its holster, it jammed the slide, making the gun useless.

Far over to the left, Chaz worked his way outward. The woods were dense and darker over this side, causing Chaz to move short distances before stopping and staring out at the monochrome grey shapes in the dark, listening for the telltale sounds of movement.

Where the hell are you?

Just when he was thinking there was nobody out there, he heard the faint crack of twigs snapping under foot from somewhere behind him.

Shit, he's been tracking me!

Chaz rolled around to the other side of the tree trunk, pushing himself into it side-on, minimising any protrusion on either side as Goran opened fire with his automatic rifle. Bark, wood chips and bullets splintered off, flying either side of Chaz's head as he fought the natural reaction to flinch, move or run. The second he heard Goran's rifle click empty, Chaz spun around the gouged tree trunk, his handgun up and firing into the dark as he tried to get the kill shot on Goran. Muzzle flashes and bullets whizzed back out of the darkness as both men moved silently between the trees in a deadly game of cat and mouse. Muzzle flashes again, from ten metres to the left of the last position, its aim in the same direction as before. Only this time, Chaz wasn't there. He was off to one side, waiting for his moment. Locking onto his target, Chaz fired off the last of his rounds. He heard a grunt and breaking twigs as something heavy hit the ground. With no pause in movement, Chaz had dropped the gun and charged full pelt across the short distance, diving on Goran as he reached for his dropped handgun with his left hand, his right arm laying useless beside him, blood leaking out from Chaz's bullet that had cut his radio in two on its way through his shoulder. Chaz punched Goran in his already painfully broken nose before grabbing the gun and shoving it up under Goran's chin.

'Go on, fucking do it, you bastard,' spat Goran in hateful, broken English, his teeth showing and eyes burning in the darkness.

'Oh no, mate, you don't get out of it that easily,' said Chaz, whipping the gun to one side before cracking it hard on Goran's temple, knocking him out cold.

***

Over the other side of the woods, Luka froze at the sounds of gunfire.

'Goran, come in.'

'I've got one of them pinned down,' came Goran's voice over his earpiece.

'Kill him and continue after the girl.'

'Da.'

Turning deeper into the woods, Luka doubled back the way he came. He knew Danny was out there. He'd gone against the edge of the woods on purpose, knowing the reflective light from the snow on the ground beyond the woods would light him up as he moved from tree to tree. With his rifle slung across his back, Luka drew his father's hunting knife and moved silently towards the last place he'd seen the shadowy figure of Danny tracking him. His earpiece let out a loud crackle as he peered between the evergreen leaves of a holly bush, following the outline of Danny as he moved behind the trunk of a large tree a few metres ahead of him.

'Goran, come in,' he whispered.

When he got no answer, he flicked the earpiece out of his ear and moved towards the tree, his upper body tense, ready to stab and slash, his legs bent, treading carefully. When he got within a few feet, he inhaled deeply, breathing out and releasing all the power in his legs in a lightning move around the tree, stabbing into thin air where Danny should have been. Confusion only crossed his face for a split second. He threw his back against the tree and searched the monochrome greyness ahead of him for movement. Leaves floated down onto his head, making him look up as they brushed his face on its way to the ground. Two eyes and gritted teeth appeared in the darkness above him as Danny opened his eyes and dropped from above, grabbing Luka's wrist to keep the knife out of the way as he flattened Luka to the ground.

Before his back sunk into the snow, Luka was on the defensive, punching Danny in the side and darting his head in as he tried to get a headbutt in. Sucking up the blow to the kidneys, Danny dodged the headbutt and slammed the back of Luka's hand repeatedly against the tree trunk until the knife flew off into the undergrowth. Another painful blow hit Danny in the side before Luka brought his knee up with such force it knocked Danny off him.

Winded, Danny got to his feet, as did Luka. The two men faced each other in the dark, the light from the moon making the whites of their eyes visible as they locked onto each other in an intense stare. Luka immediately swung the rifle on his back around, his snow-covered fingers fumbling to get a grip and find the trigger. Danny launched himself forward, rugby tackling Luka, sending both of them crashing through the bushes and out of the wood, dropping onto a flat, snow covered surface.

A moment of confusion passed through their minds, as the surface they hit was as hard as concrete beneath the thin layer of snow. The rifle rattling away as both men slid apart. The realisation they were lying on a frozen lake, hitting them at the same time. They jumped upright, their feet sliding as they stood uneasily facing each other, both men with faces like granite and eyes locked murderously on each other. Both men having to believe they were better than the other; if they didn't, they were dead already.

45

Armed units approached the farmhouse en masse, hurtling past the burning van in the courtyard before sweeping into the farmhouse and barn in well-rehearsed formations.

'Living room clear, two men down, no sign of Pearson or the others.'

'Affirmative.'

'First floor clear, three men down up here, plus one on the stairs, no sign of Pearson or the others.'

'All unit's keep clear of the kitchen, Two Hostile dead and some sort of noxious gas from a pan on the hob. Hobbs is going in with a gas mask to isolate the source.'

The radio talk continued to come in until the property was searched and secured and called in. Less than a minute later, vehicles flooded into the courtyard, fanning out and sliding to a stop. Simon's driver hopped out and trudged through the snow to open the door. Simon got out, his face lacking its usual jovial appearance as he marched into the farmhouse.

'Status?'

'Sergeant Foster's unit are all dead, sir. We've found multiple footprints heading into the trees from the rear of the farmhouse.'

'Thank you, Lieutenant. How quickly can we get a helicopter here, full thermal cameras?' said Simon, turning his nose up at the slight remnants of gas from the boiled-dry pan of bleach and ammonium based cleaner.

'Already en route, sir. ETA is six minutes.'

'Thank you, Lieutenant. Proceed with the search upon its arrival,' said Simon, coming to a halt at Sergeant Foster's bullet-ridden body on the living room floor. His face flashed with anger for a moment before he forced it back down and regained composure.

'Yes sir,' replied the lieutenant, leaving the room to organise his men.

Simon walked out of the farmhouse into the courtyard. He looked at the burning van with the charred M134 Gatling gun mounted in the back before putting his phone to his ear, turning to take in the devastation as it rang.

'Jenkins.'

'Edward, I would say good evening, but it's not. They took the bait as hoped, but turned up in force. It looks like a war zone down here. All Sergeant Foster's men are dead,' said Simon, his tone unusually melancholy.

'I see. What about Daniel, his men, and Miss Wallace?'

'We are as yet unsure. I've got air support with a thermal camera en route to search the surrounding woods.'

'Let's keep our fingers crossed. What's the next move?'

'Pull Hake and Utting, keep them on ice, no phone calls, no contact with the outside world. I don't want Montgomery or Benedict to know we've got them. I need more on Arthur Montgomery before I see the PM, because I'm going to need his approval before we detain him. With Montgomery's connections, we're going to need more than a few circumstantial phone calls to hold him. We still have nothing to connect Vincent Benedict to Arthur Montgomery or to say he's the Wolf.'

'I'll put everyone on it, movements, financials, old relationships, ex-employees. There has to be a weak link, there always is,' Edward said.

'Thank you, Edward. I appreciate your support as always. I'll call you as soon as I have news,' Simon said, ending the call and pocketing the phone before looking into the night sky, the sound of the distant whomp of rotor blades announcing the incoming helicopter.

46

Loud cracks and pings reverberated through the ice beneath their feet. Danny and Luka's eyes flicked off each other towards the rifle lying closer to the middle of the lake. They flicked back a split second later, each reading the other's body language, noting the tensing of the legs and deep breaths. As if set off by a starter's pistol, both men exploded into a sprint, their feet sliding as they fought for grip in the rush for the rifle. The ice made a cacophony of cracks, pops and pings as it protested at the weight pounding across its surface. Being smaller and lighter than Danny, Luka reached the weapon first, sliding down on one knee to scoop it up ahead of him. Danny's hand grabbed the barrel as he spun on the ice, pushing it skyward as the muzzle flashed and rounds whizzed off into the night sky.

While both still gripping the rifle, they continued to punch, knee and kick each other. Danny yanked the rifle down towards the ground, pulling Luka's finger back on the trigger and sending bullets punching deep into the ice. Only when the magazine emptied and silence returned did both men freeze, still gripping each other tightly, rooted to the spot at the increasing cracking sound that was spreading outwards from their feet. Their eyes flicked down to the ice and back up at each other a split second before they dropped like stones into the icy waters beneath.

As the rifle disappeared below them, Danny fought against cold water shock. Instead of panicking for the surface, he kicked out against Luka, pushing him deeper before swimming for the moonlit hole in the ice above him. As his fingers felt the cold night air, an arm curled around his neck, dragging him back down.

Luka gripped him like a vice, punching him in the ribs with his other hand to force the air out and drown him, before his own burning lungs forced him to make a break for the surface. His plan was working; Danny's head was spinning and his lungs burned for breath. He jabbed his elbows back into Luka's torso time and time again, to no avail. With the point of passing out fast approaching, Danny moved both his arms up and behind him and locked his fingers around the back of Luka's head. Feeling with his thumbs, he found the pressure points at the top of the jaw and just below the ears. Danny pushed his thumbs in with all his might, causing Luka to thrash and jerk in intense pain. He continued to keep a grip around Danny's neck for a few more seconds before the pain forced him to let go. Letting go, Danny spun around and kicked Luka away, watching bubbles erupt from Luka's silent scream as he put his hands to his ears and sunk out of sight, swallowed up in the inky blackness.

A wave of panic hit Danny as he swam up and hit solid ice. He slapped the underside with his palms, desperately searching for the way out. His body started convulsing as the last remnants of air left his lungs. Danny's eyes rolled back in his head. A numbness beyond the cold took over as calm washed over him. Somewhere, in what remained of his consciousness, he heard gunshots and hammering. Chaz pulled Danny up and out of the hole he'd shot and frantically hammered through with the heel of his boot. He pulled him across the ice by his arms, lying him safely on the bank. When he got no pulse, Chaz started CPR. The loud whomp of helicopter blades deafened him as it appeared from over the woods, its powerful search light circling Chaz as he worked on Danny's chest.

'Come on, you stubborn bastard, breathe,' Chaz yelled over the noise as he continued CPR.

Like someone flicking on a switch, Danny jerked, coughing out a mouthful of water, before sucking in a massive lungful of air as Simon's men emerged from the woods and rushed over.

'It's ok, he's breathing,' Chaz shouted, putting Danny on his side in the recovery position as he continued to breathe, cough and splutter before finally throwing up. After a minute, he found the strength to push himself up and sit. Staring across at the lake, shaking uncontrollably as his eyes searched for any sign of Luka.

It was too dark to see the far side of the lake and the footsteps leading out into the woods. Nor could he see Luka's hateful eyes looking back at him from behind the tree line. Unzipping the pocket on his soaking tactical vest and pulled a phone out, thankful for the water resistant rating as it came into life in his shivering touch.

'It's me, you said to call you if it didn't go to plan. Well, it didn't go to plan.'

'Where are you?'

'The woods behind the farmhouse. There's a road two miles south of here. Be on it,' Luka said, shaking uncontrollably.

'Ok,'

'Bring dry clothes and hurry before I freeze to death.'

'On my way.'

The phone went dead. Luka watched the helicopter move off to the far side of the woods. Before he could go, he had to do one thing. He tracked around the lake under cover of the trees until he was at the point where he and Danny had crashed through the hedge onto the lake. Getting down on his knees, he felt around in the disturbed snow until his fingers touched his father's hunting knife. 'I promise you will see his blood,' he whispered to himself before sliding it back into its sheath.

Luka headed off at a fast pace. One, to put some distance between him and the lake, and two, to get the blood moving and some warmth back into his body. He headed south as fast as he could go, only stopping to bury himself under the snow when the helicopter circled overhead, its thermal camera failing to pick up his heat signature under the freezing layer. Once he heard it move off, Luka threw off the snow and made his way to the road. After five freezing minutes hiding in the hedge, the lights of a car appeared in the distance. It stopped where it was and flashed the lights twice. Luka emerged from the hedge and stood facing it until it moved up to him.

'You're late,' Luka said, throwing his knife on the passenger seat and stripping off his soaking clothes, pulling on dry ones before getting into the car.

'I stopped on the way. Thought you might appreciate one of these,' Vincent Benedict said, passing Luka one of the hot lattes from the cup holder in the centre console.

Luka took it without answering, tipping the cup back in his shaky hands to gulp the hot coffee down.

'We need to move things along. The hope of containment is lost. It's time for damage limitation and self preservation before they have time to get ahead of us,' Vincent said, accelerating the powerful car down the road.

'And after I do this?'

'Our business will be concluded, and your account credited with the agreed sum.'

'And you?'

'Contingencies are in place. It's time to leave for pastures new. I have a position for a man like yourself, if you're interested.'

'We finish our current business, then we talk. Now turn up the heater, I'm freezing.'

47

The clean up at the farmhouse took its toll on morale. They drove Goran away with an armed escort this time, while Simon orchestrated his men with sombre professionalism. A team searched the woods while another removed the bodies from the farmhouse, placing the black body bags in plain black coroners vans.

It was getting close to dawn by the time Danny and the others got back to the house in Muswell Hill. Apart from being thankful to be alive, nobody was in the mood for light conversation, opting to retire to bed instead. Danny threw off the blankets they'd wrapped him in since being fished out of the lake and jumped in the shower. He cranked it to the hottest setting he could stand, until the smell of pond water and the cold he felt to his core was rinsed from his body. Mind and body exhausted, he climbed into the army cot bed and was asleep in minutes. His eyes pinged open, and he sat bolt upright a few minutes later, staring at the daylight shining around the curtains. He looked at his watch in confusion, finally realising it wasn't minutes later, but past eleven the next morning. Running his hands through his unruly mop of hair, he dressed and made his way downstairs to the kitchen.

'Oh, heads up, Cinderella's awake,' said Smudge as Danny entered.

Amanda and Chaz's heads turned from the table to look at him.

'Alright guys, anyone want one?' Danny said, heading for the coffee machine.

Smudge and Amanda held up full coffee mugs and shook their heads while Chaz got up and joined Danny.

'You alright, mate? For a minute there I thought I lost you,' Chaz said quietly.

'You and me both, mate. Thanks for being there.'

'Don't mention it. I couldn't let you leave me on my own with Fergus and dopey bollocks over there, could I?' Chaz said with a grin.

'Oi, I heard that,' Smudge grumbled from his chair.

'So what's been going on around here?' Danny asked.

'You missed all the excitement while you were asleep. After that disastrous shitstorm yesterday, Simon and Edward had everyone up all night looking into Arthur Montgomery and Vincent Benedict. About eight o'clock this morning Edward's lot found CCTV footage of Montgomery's Bentley entering a north London car park the night Fergus got shot. Five minutes later, the same Audi Q7 used to bust out the guy from the hospital entered the car park. They parked in a part not covered by the car park cameras, but what they didn't know is there's a new high definition camera mounted on a building society across the road. It's got a partial view into the car park and its 4k resolution is so good, Edward's guys expanded and enhanced it enough to see the two mercenaries from the hospital pulling up next to Montgomery's Bentley. The driver lowers the window and hands Amanda's bag from the old factory to Montgomery. It even shows Montgomery getting the photos and notebook out of the bag before turning the interior light on to have a good look. Shortly after that, both vehicles leave. Because of the sensitivity with Montgomery being a government advisor and Vincent Benedict about to be appointed Foreign Minister, Simon left early to get the Prime Ministers approval to arrest them.'

'Yeah, they'll be picking Montgomery up right about now,' Smudge chipped in.

'Good, what about Vincent Benedict?'

'They haven't found anything on him yet, but they're still digging. Anyway, once they've got Montgomery, they can put the pressure on him to spill the beans on Benedict.'

'Let's hope so. What about the guy you nailed in the woods and his mate in the lake?' Danny said to Chaz.

'They've identified him as a Goran Petrovic, ex-Serbian Special Forces. He's a mercenary wanted by Interpol in three countries. Tough bastard, lips sealed tighter than a duck's butt. They won't get anything out of him. Interpol thinks your friend from the lake is his old commander, Luka Horvat. They'll be able to confirm it once the divers find the body.'

'A few more seconds under that ice and they'd have been looking for my body as well. At least it looks like we're getting closer to going home and forgetting all about this crap,' Danny said, draining his mug.

'Amen to that, although Ferg would probably say he'd like a few more weeks in the hospital away from Gaynor and the kids,' Smudge said, chuckling, before turning to give a reassuring smile and wink to Amanda.

She smiled back, her eyes looking warmly into Smudge's as she put her hand on his leg, which didn't go unnoticed by Danny and Chaz, who looked at each other with raised eyebrows.

'Amanda and Smudge, I didn't see that coming,' Danny said, looking back at Smudge putting his hand on top of hers.

'Me neither, must be his witty intellectual conversation,' said Chaz with a wide grin.

The two of them turned at Whiskins entering the room.

'Hi guys, the boss just called. They've arrested Arthur Montgomery and surveillance says Vincent Benedict left the country on his yacht in the early hours of this morning. So there's no further reason for you to be here. If you'd like to get your stuff together, Harrison will run you all home.'

'Suits me,' said Danny, draining his cup.

48

After leaving the meeting with the Prime Ministers approval, Simon led three cars through London to Arthur Montgomery's six bedroom townhouse in the affluent St John's Wood area of London. With no markings, no lights or wailing sirens, the cars pulled up on the road outside the impressive property. A dozen suited MI5 agents got out and followed Simon up to the closed barred gates. Montgomery's Bentley sat parked on the drive beyond. Simon pressed the intercom button on the pillar by the gate and waited patiently for a reply. When none came, he gave a nod to one of his men, who operated a frequency scanner until the gates responded and opened smoothly inwards. The men went in ahead of Simon, heading for the front door, not running but walking fast with a sense of purpose. The two nearest the Bentley pointed out the blown-in driver's window on the far side. A closer look showed Montgomery's driver lying across the front seats, a neat hole in his temple where a bullet had entered and a crater on the other side where it had exited, covering the soft cream leather interior in blood, bone and bits of brain. Simon reached in and touched the driver's hand. He was still warm and the blood hadn't started oxidising into a rusty brown yet.

'It's fresh. They could still be here.'

The approach of his men changed in an instant. Guns were drawn, bodies moved away from the windows and backs slid against the brickwork of the house as they approached the front door in well-rehearsed formation.

***

'You guys ready?' said Harrison, swinging a set of car keys around by the keyring.

'Yeah, good to go,' said Danny, grabbing his old kit bag, closely followed by Chaz, Smudge and Amanda.

They got into the company Land Rover and drove smoothly out of the automatic gates. Whiskins watched them go on the monitor inside. He pressed the button to close the gate behind them and picked up his mobile. Typing quickly, he hit send and returned to his desk to run through more data on Arthur Montgomery. Back in the car, Chaz sat forward in his seat at the sight of an upcoming Tube station.

'Actually, drop us off here, Harrison. I think I'll get the Tube and see how Fergus is doing.'

'Tell Sicknote I'll come and see him tomorrow,' Danny said, as Chaz stepped out of the car.

'Yeah, that goes for me too,' Smudge shouted after

him.

'Ok, and Amanda, nice meeting you. Don't trust a word that comes out of Smudge's mouth, ok?' Chaz added with a grin.

'Ok, bye Chaz,' she replied with the first relaxed smile he'd seen since this whole nightmare started.

'Right, next stop—your place,' Harrison said to Danny, pulling back into the flow of traffic.

***

'On three, one, two, three. Go, go, go!'

Two of Simon's agents swung an enforcer battering ram at the lock on the front door, blowing it inwards in a shower of splintered door frame pieces. At the same time, an agent put a bullet through the toughened glass sliding door at the rear of the house, shattering the twin panels of glass into a million crystals. He stood back to let a four-man team enter through the empty frame. With another four-man team entering the front, they split into pairs, calmly sounding off as they cleared one room after another.

Outside, Simon heard, 'Suspect found in the downstairs office, DOA, bullet wound to the head,' over his earpiece.

'Shit,' he said to himself without attempting to enter the house. There was no point, there would be no evidence. Whoever did this was long gone. Turning his back to the house, he pulled his mobile and called Edward.

'Simon.'

'Montgomery's dead, bullet to the head.'

'Christ, that's going to cause a lot of awkward questions in the cabinet.'

'That's the least of my problems. What did you get out of Hake and Utting?' Simon asked, changing the subject.

'They're still being cagey, hanging on for a deal. What is clear is they know nothing about Vincent Benedict. Montgomery was their only point of contact.'

'Ok, keep on them, I'll be back soon.'

'Oh, just one other thing,' Edward said before Simon could hang up.

'Yes?'

'A bit of a puzzle really. Both Hake and Utting swear blind that they didn't give Montgomery the address of the farmhouse. They say Montgomery killed the contact number before they found out. He never sent them a new number.'

'So how did they know where it was, and how did they know what manpower they needed to attack it?' Simon said, more running the information through his head than asking Edward.

'Who else knew?' Edward replied.

'No one, just you and me, and my team at the house. My God, one of the team is working for them. Meet me at the house, I'll call ahead. Nobody leaves until I get there.'

'Ok, I'm on my way,' said Edward, hanging up.

Simon was straight back on the phone to the house in

Muswell Hill.

'Sir.'

'Who's this?'

'Whiskins, sir.'

'Whiskins, is everyone back at the house?'

'Yes sir, they're all back.'

'Good.'

'Apart from Harrison, he's taking Miss Wallace and Mr Pearson's lot home, as you instructed.'

'What do you mean, as I instructed?'

'Er, Harrison said you called to say Montgomery had been arrested, and Vincent Benedict had fled the country, so they weren't needed. He took the Land Rover to take them home.'

'Jesus, it's Harrison. Bring up the tracker location on the Land Rover. Harrison could be leading them into a trap.'

'Hang on,' Whiskins said, his fingers dancing across the keyboard to bring up the vehicle's location. 'That can't be right.'

'What is it, Whiskins?'

'Location not found. It was last seen here at ten fifteen this morning,' Whiskins said, leaning across to open Harrison's desk drawer. 'Sir, I've just found the vehicle tracker in Harrison's desk drawer.'

'Christ, get everyone on traffic cams and then put the number plate into the ANPR system. I'll call Pearson and try to warn him.'

'Yes sir,' Whiskins said, hanging up the phone. A flicker of a smile crept across his face before he turned serious and addressed the team. 'Listen up, the boss wants Harrison found. It's possible he's working for the enemy and leading Pearson and the others into a trap. We have to find him and find him now.'

The shocked faces of the team fell back into work mode as they hit the computers and started searching for the car Harrison took.

49

Harrison pulled up smoothly outside Danny's house in Walthamstow. Danny looked at it with thoughts of a hot bath, to chase away the occasional shivers he was still getting from his near drowning in the lake, a warm change of clothes, possibly followed by a beer, TV, and a snooze on the sofa. He also had a yearning to talk to his girlfriend, Nikki, in Australia.

'Thanks, Harrison,' he said, turning in the seat to look at Smudge and Amanda in the back. They were sitting close, with Amanda's hand resting on Smudge's thigh. 'You kids have fun. I call you about visiting Fergus tomorrow, Smudge.'

'Ok boss,' Smudge said with a grin.

'Bye, Danny, and thank you for everything,' Amanda said.

Danny just smiled, grabbed his bag, and stepped out of the vehicle. He was happy for Smudge. Still smiling, he took the two steps across the pavement to the tiled path that led to his front door. As his foot hit the floor, his smile dropped. The hairs on the back of his neck stood on end. Something in his subconscious triggered a threat. He could hear a car approaching the Range Rover. As he turned, his eyes locked with Luka's in the passenger seat, his arm hanging out the window, his hand holding something dark and disc-like. Danny's eyes flicked to the driver, taking in the million-dollar smile of Vincent Benedict, the Wolf.

All this happened in the blink of an eye. By the time Danny got one foot back the way he came, the car flew past the Land Rover. Luka reached out when they were side by side, letting the powerful magnetic pull of the explosive device grab onto the Land Rover with a loud clunk. Danny locked on Harrison and Amanda's confused faces as they tried to process why he was hurtling back towards the car, and what the loud clunk on the far side of the car was. Smudge knew something was up. He instinctively released his seat belt and reached across Amanda, his hand heading for the door lever.

On the outside, Danny's fingers barely touched the handle as the device went off, his mind locking a snapshot of Amanda's panicked face next to Smudge's understanding look. Unable to hold on to the image any longer, Danny's mind pressed play, and the snapshot was wiped away by a fireball that consumed the car. The simultaneous explosion was earth shattering, ripping the car apart. Its shockwave blowing the rear passenger door clean off its hinges, sending it, and Danny flying through the air into the front door, the sheer force of his impact blowing the door inwards like he was a human battering ram.

He lay on his back unmoving, the sleeve of his jacket still smouldering as blood spread across the tiled hallway from underneath his singed hair. It found the grout lines and travelled away fast, like tiny trains hurtling to multiple destinations. In the street, glass and powdered snow twinkled to the floor from every house and car window, the blast wave taking out every pane and shaking the roofs for twenty metres in all directions. When the boom died away, a cacophony of car alarms took its place, shrieking at each other out of time, in different pitches.

50

Ceiling tiles moved across in front of his vision, broken up every fifth tile by a bright light. He heard voices talking fast, but he couldn't understand what they were saying. The sound of wheels clicked along a tiled floor. Confusion clouded his mind. Nothing made sense. What was going on? No pain, no anger, no memory of what had happened, just numbness. He closed his eyes, embracing the feeling of drifting away.

'Mr Pearson, try to stay awake for me. Daniel, can you open your eyes for me?'

'Just let me sleep.'

A kind face with a smile looked down at him, the ceiling still moving above her.

'My name is Emma Taylor. You've had an accident. I'm a doctor. I'm going to take good care of you, ok? Daniel. Daniel. Try to keep awake for me.'

'I don't want to fight anymore. I just want to sleep.'

His vision blurred and darkness pulled in around the

edges until the world went black. He could hear Emma talking frantically, as if from a great distance.

'Daniel, Daniel. Blood pressure's dropping, we're losing him. Let's get him into theatre. Call the crash team. NOW.'

***

'He's coming round. Call someone, Scott.'

'Yes, of course, absolutely. Hello? Anyone? He's awake,' Scott called out through the door to the private hospital room.

'Danny, can you hear me?' Nikki said, concern written on her face as he looked at her vaguely, a frown forming across his forehead. 'Oh god, he doesn't recognise me. Danny, it's me, your girlfriend, Nikki. You remember? Scott's sister,' she continued, talking fast as she tried to keep a lid on her fears.

Danny stared at her, his frown turning into a look of confusion. After what seemed an age, he opened his mouth. 'I know who you are, you daft bugger. How are you here? You were in Australia when I text you this morning.'

'Oh honey, that was five weeks ago,' Nikki said, moving to one side to let a doctor check on him.

'Good morning, Mr Pearson, glad to see you back with us. Can you just look at me? Great. Follow my finger, great. Any blurred vision, headaches?'

'No, head feels a little fuzzy though.'

'You may get that and headaches or blurred vision for a while. Do you know who you are, your date of birth?'

'Yes, how did I get here?' Danny said back abruptly.

'What's the last thing you remember?'

'Texting Nikki to say I was going home. Then, er, I don't know,' Danny fell silent, trying to remember. A blinding flash of pain hit him from behind the eyes. The image of Amanda and Smudge looking helplessly at him through the car window before being consumed by a massive fireball flashed across his mind, as real as if he'd travelled back to that point in time.

'Ok, take it easy, breathe through it, Mr Pearson.'

The pain slowly died away. Danny took his head out of his hands and opened his eyes. 'Smudge and Amanda are dead.'

'I'm afraid they are, Mr Pearson. You sustained a head injury which caused swelling and a bleed on the brain. We had to operate to stop the bleed and sedate you until the swelling went down. You had an MRI scan this morning, which all looks good, so we decided to bring you round. You're lucky to be alive.'

'I've been told that once or twice.'

The doctor continued with some more tests while Nikki held Danny's hand and Scott sat in the chair in the room's corner, waiting patiently for the doctor to finish and leave.

'You gave us quite a fright,' Nikki said, leaning in to give him a kiss.

'Yes, old man, so glad you didn't die on me. There's a rather large garage bill with your name on it for the repair of my car. Apparently, my insurance company doesn't cover me for loaning it to a bunch of lunatics, or for damage from automatic weapons. Can't imagine why not,' Scott said with a smile.

'What's that, Scott? Sorry, mate, brain damage. I don't remember that at all,' Danny replied, tapping his head and grinning.

'My dear fellow, you have to have a brain in the first place for it to be damaged.'

'Two minutes awake and you two are at it already. You gave us quite a scare. I thought I'd lost you,' Nikki said, her eyes misting up as a single tear rolled down her cheek.

He moved his hand up to wipe it away, stopping halfway to move his hands to his own head as another flash of pain coursed through it. The image of Amanda and Smudge returned. The fireball consuming them gave way to an image of his wife and child before their deaths. That tumbled into the image of an ex-girlfriend, Alice, disappearing into the crowd at Victoria train station, led to her death by Lars Silverman. That tumbled into Kate, another woman he'd loved, killed at the hands of a Chinese assassin. Unable to breathe or move, Danny rode out the images as they flicked and tumbled back to Amanda and Smudge. Their faces faded away to be replaced by the image of Luka and Vincent Benedict's million-dollar smile, looking at him from the passing car seconds before the explosion, fading to the image of Nikki and the hospital room. The pain rolled away and his body allowed him to move and breathe. He gasped and panted, as if trapped underwater. Nikki hugged him, then moved away and put her hands to his face. It took him a few seconds to realise she was wiping away the tears from his eyes.

'Er, I'll just go and get a coffee. Leave you two alone for a bit. Sorry about your friend Smudge, old boy,' Scott said awkwardly before slipping out the door.

51

Danny heard Fergus and Chaz heading through the ward before they entered the room. He grinned at hearing the nurse tell them that Mr Pearson was not to have alcohol.

'Course not love, that would be very irresponsible of us,' Fergus said unconvincingly.

'I mean it, no alcohol, and please refrain from calling me love,' the nurse snapped back.

'Alright, I got it, no alcohol, and don't worry sweet cheeks, I won't call you love any more.'

'Friends of yours?' Nikki said, seeing Danny chuckle.

'More than friends, family,' Danny said as Chaz and Fergus's grinning faces poked around the door.

'Oh fuck Chaz, it's hideous, his face, it's all disfigured by the explosion.'

'Nah mate, he's always been that ugly,' Chaz chuckled back.

'Very funny, alright guys. When did you get out of

hospital Ferg?'

'Last week, just in time for Smudge's funeral. Sorry you missed it mate.'

The room fell into an awkward silence for a few seconds before Chaz piped up.

'Well, whose this pretty young thing Daniel? Aren't you going to introduce us?'

'Like you don't know, this is Nikki. Nikki, this is Chaz and the one with the beers is Fergus,' Danny said, catching a can and cracking it open.

'Pleased to meet you,' Nikki said with a smile.

'Punching above your weight there mate. You're Scott's sister, right?'

'That's right.'

'Not possible. She's got to be adopted,' said Fergus.

'Got to be,' agreed Chaz.

'I was expecting Scott in a wig,' Fergus said

'Yeah, you're way too good looking to be related to Scott,' said Chaz

'Er, thanks, I think,' Nikki said, taking a beer from Fergus's outstretched hand.

'So when are you getting out of here? The old noggins all ok, yeah?' Chaz said.

'Tomorrow, and yes, the noggins all ok. I still remember you owe me twenty quid,' Danny said with a grin.

'Shut up and have another beer. You'll soon forget about that,' Fergus said, chucking another can in Danny's direction.

They talked and laughed for a while, raising the last

cans in a salute to Smudge and Amanda. The noise bringing the nurse in, who swiftly told them Danny needed rest, not beer, and they should go. After protesting, then trying to get her phone number, Chaz and Fergus offered Nikki a lift back to Scott's, and they all departed. Danny watched some TV until the beer ran its natural course and he needed to pee. He went into the ensuite bathroom. When he came out Simon was sitting in a chair against the wall. He sat relaxed, his legs crossed in his immaculate Savile row suite, his hand resting in his lap.

'Mr Pearson,' he said calmly.

'I wondered when you'd show up,' Danny said, sitting on the side of the bed.

'There wasn't much point until you where awake, was there,' Simon said in his usual jovial manor.

'I see there's nothing about Montgomery or Benedict in the news,' Danny said, pointing at the TV.

'Good god no, a corrupt government advisor and gunrunning, drug dealing Foreign Secretary with an MBE, far too embarrassing for the government. The spin doctors invented a rather convincing south London terrorist cell for the recent shootings and the bombing of the car. The media lapped it up.'

'Did you get much out of Arthur Montgomery?'

'Montgomery? Oh, of course Harrison led you into the trap before we got back. No, we didn't get anything out of Montgomery. He was dead when we got there. Vincent Benedict had him killed to close the last link back to him.'

'Have you got Benedict yet?' Danny said, his eyes narrowing and face hardening as his mood darkened.

'No, officially we have nothing on him. We tracked him to the Camen islands, where he moved all his funds around. Then he moved around some of the more dubious African countries, more arms deals presumably. We think he is somewhere in the Middle East.' Simon said, examining his neatly manicured nails as he spoke.

'Hang on, what did you say?'

'He's somewhere in—.'

'No, no, you said Harrison lead us into the trap?' Danny said

'Yes, Harrison told you I called to say Montgomery had been arrested and Vincent Benedict had fled the country, and he was to take you home,' Simon said, confused by the back track.

'No, that's wrong. Whiskins told us he'd taken the call. It was him who told Harrison you wanted him to take us home. He set us up, not Harrison.'

'You're sure,' Simon said, wondering if Danny's brain injury had impaired his memory.

'Do I look like I'm not sure,' Danny growled back angrily.

'No, you do not. I must go. Take care of yourself, Mr Pearson,' Simon said, getting up to leave.

'Simon,' Danny said as he headed out the door.

Simon stopped in the doorway and looked back at him.

'I want him, the Wolf. When you find him, I want him, for Smudge and Amanda,' Danny said, his eyes dark and focused, his face taut, hard as stone.

'Your are not the only one to lose good friends over this. Get well Mr Pearson. I'll be in touch.'

Simon left the room, the door swinging slowly shut behind him, leaving Danny alone with his anger and his thoughts.

52

After a couple of weeks at Scott's, Danny and Nikki headed across London. The snow had melted away, and they made good time reaching Danny's freshly repaired house. They pulled up, parking on top of a newly repaired patch of tarmac, the only reminder of the destroyed Land Rover.

'You ok,' Nikki said, noticing Danny looking at his house, hesitating to get out of the car.

He remained quiet for a couple of second, before taking a big sigh. 'Yeah, I'm ok,' he finally said, giving her a smile as he opened the car door.

Danny spotted his neighbour, Mr Maynard, from across the road and gave him a friendly wave. Mr Maynard just frowned back before ducking inside his house, slamming the front door behind him.

'Nice neighbours,' Nikki said.

'Mmm, I can't blame him. Let's just say this isn't the first time I've blown up the neighbourhood,' Danny said, walking past her to his front door.

'Wait, what? Not the first time?' Nikki said, hurrying after him.

Danny unlocked his new front door and went inside, pausing just for a second to look down at the clean tiled floor before heading to the kitchen.

'We better get some pizzas ordered. The guys will be here in a bit,' Danny said, picking up the phone.

'Oh no, you don't change the subject. I want to know about the other times,' Nikki said.

Danny stopped what he was doing, turned, he slid his arms around Nikki, picking her up off the ground to kiss her passionately on the lips while she wrapped her legs around him.

'Forget what's happened in the past. This is now. You're my now. How about I sell this place, get rid of all the bad memories? You sell your place and we get somewhere together, either here or in Australia. I don't care.'

Nikki looked into his eyes and beamed, then kissed him again. 'Really.'

'Yes, really,' Danny said, smiling back.

'Oi, oi, put her down man,' shouted Chaz, walking in through the open door, closely followed by Fergus and a crate of beer, his wife Gaynor and Smudge's sister Kelly.

'Come in guys, I was just about to order pizza,' Danny said, putting Nikki down to greet them.

The afternoon went well and drifted into evening. They ate and drank, raising a drink in sombre memory to Smudge before laughing as they reminisced over

Smudge's past antics. Danny got up and went through to the kitchen. He grabbed another can of beer from the fridge, putting it down on the sink to look at his buzzing phone and read the message.

"*Outside.*"

Danny opened the fridge again and grabbed the six-pack of beers, turned and put them in the cupboard under the sink before heading for the front door. He glanced into the living room on his way.

'We're out of beers. I'm just popping down the off-licence, won't be long.'

He got a casual ok from Nikki, without breaking conversation with Gaynor and Kelly. Chaz and Fergus picked up something in his tone and turned to face him. Danny flicked his eyes toward the girls and gave an almost indistinguishable shake of the head. Chaz and Fergus gave the tiniest nod back and continued talking. Danny walked up his path and looked up and down the street, Simons car sat a little way back, just out of view from the house. Simon's driver, Michael, got out as he approached and moved around the car to open the rear passenger door.

'Mr Pearson,' Simon said, sitting relaxed on the opposite side of the rear seat, a large A4 envelope on his lap.

'What have you got for me?' Danny said bluntly.

'Very well, we'll dispense with the niceties and get straight down to it. We've found your man.'

'Vincent Benedict?'

'As it turns out, no. The real Vincent Benedict

disappeared ten years ago, no family, no ties. We believe our man targeted him as they look alike, killed him and stole his identity, before ingratiating himself with certain influential members of parliament. Anyway, after running DNA from his flat through various multinational databases, we found out the Wolf's real name is Klaus Meyer, educated in England, son of Hans Meyer, the leader of a notorious German criminal organisation and his English ex-model wife. Klaus disappears after the authorities shut the organisation down and sent his father to prison, two years before taking Benedict's identity.'

'Fascinating. Where the fuck is he?' Danny growled impatiently.

'Patience, Mr Pearson, before I get to that, I have to make you aware of the situation. This whole escapade, if it were to get out, would be extremely damaging to this country. Montgomery and Benedict effectively duped the government, and the monarchy for that matter. There are people in high places shitting their Savile Row trousers at the thought of this becoming public, with that in mind, I have been given the green light to take care of the situation, quietly, no official orders, no paperwork and total deniability on their part.'

'Where is he?' Danny repeated, unimpressed.

'In Somalia, as a guest of Abshir Ibraham, he's the leader of a splinter group, split off from the Al-Shabab Jihadists. Apparently, they hate everything the west stands for, unless you happen to be the one selling them the latest weapons. The details are all in here. Be at

London airport for 10 a.m. on Monday, I've chartered a jet to fly you to Wajir Airport in neighbouring Kenya. One of my local agents will meet you. He'll take you across the border into Somalia under the cover of darkness. Let me know what equipment you need and I'll make sure it's there for your arrival. The flight back will leave Wajir Airport at 1p.m. Wednesday evening. Be on it Mr Pearson, there won't be another one.' Simon said, handing the envelope to Danny. 'If you wouldn't mind, Michael.'

The driver got out and moved around the car once more, opening the door for Danny.

'Good luck, Mr Pearson,' Simon said as he got out.

53

After a quick jog down to the off licence, Danny returned to the house with a crate of beer. He popped his head into the living room and smiled at Nikki, nodding at Chaz and Fergus to follow him into the kitchen when she returned to her conversation with Kelly and Gaynor.

'What's going on?' Chaz said, sitting down at the kitchen table next to him.

'Yeah, come on, I know that look,' said Fergus, joining them.

Danny pulled the envelope from under his jacket and placed it on the table. 'I know where he is,' he said, his face hardening at the thought of Smudge.

Both Chaz and Fergus's expressions changed to match Danny's as they all looked at the envelope.

'Simon?' Chaz said, tapping the envelope.

'Simon.' Danny answered, flipping the lip to pull the contents out.

Spreading it out on the kitchen table, the three of them looked over a series of satellite pictures showing a large house sitting inside a compound wall. It was located to the north of a small town or village called Fafahdun, around seventy miles from the Kenyan border, and a hundred and twenty from Wajir Airport. There was a watchtower just inside the wall at the gated entrance, and another one in the far corner opposite. Six vehicles showed up, dotted around the property with four inside and two outside the wall, they looked to be a mixture of old 4x4's probably Toyota Land Cruisers and pickup trucks, maybe Toyota Hilux's, with .50-caliber machine gun mounts. The second picture was a much closer shot of six people sitting around a table on the roof terrace, five jihads dressed in green uniforms, machine guns propped up against the seating all around them, the sixth man was a white male, baseball cap covering most of his sandy coloured hair, you couldn't see the faces as it was taken from directly above. The next photo had been taken from the ground using a large telephoto lens. It showed the Wolf clearly, baseball cap still on his head, sunglasses hiding his eyes as he gave his million-dollar smile to the jihadi leader Abshir Ibraham sitting next to him. The last satellite picture was zoomed out, showing the property in relation to Fafahdun, and the lay of the land for a mile on either side of the property. Danny thumbed through the flight details before looking at a piece on paper with the name and cell number of the agent meeting him, and the estimated number of hostiles within the compound, which was thirty.

'When do we go?' said Fergus.

'We! No, no Ferg, I'm not asking either of you to come with me,' Danny said.

'You try stopping us and you'll end up with another dent in that thick skull of yours,' said Chaz, all faces looking fixed and determined at each other.

The room remained locked in a silent stalemate until Danny finally gave in. 'Monday morning 10 a.m. A private jet out of city airport, which gives up two days to work out a plan, and one day to get an equipment list together for the mission.'

'Mission, what mission?' said Gaynor, walking into the kitchen, her eyes immediately focusing on the satellite images on the table.

'Now, don't start love, this is something we've got to do for Smudge,' Fergus said.

'What's going on, Danny?' Nikki said, following the raise voices.

'We know where the Wolf is. We're going to get him,' Danny said bluntly, his features hard, eyes dark and determined.

'What! You're all crazy. Two of you have only been out of hospital a few weeks, you both nearly died, what's a matter with you,' Nikki said raising her voice.

'Kill him, fucking kill him. Painfully, make him suffer. Do that for me Danny, for my brother,' said Kelly, pushing past them to the table, tears rolling down her face.

'I will Kelly, we all will,' Danny said, looking up at

her.

Gaynor looked at Kelly, her mind processing what was happening. A moment later, she put her arm around Kelly and looked at Fergus. 'You kill that son of a bitch and come back to me, you hear me Fergus, come back to me.'

Fergus nodded and stood up, putting his arms around Gaynor and kelly.

'I don't know if I can do this, first Australia, then you get blown up, and now you're going off to god knows where to kill a man. I need some space. I'm going to my brothers,' Nikki said, turning away, tears in her eyes.

Danny watched her leave the kitchen, saying nothing. The front door slamming a minute later. He eventually drew a deep breath and turned his attention back to the table.

'Gaynor, take Kelly home, will you. We've got work to do.'

Gaynor looked to Fergus, who nodded to indicate she should do as Danny said.

'Ok, come on Kelly, let's leave them to it.'

Fergus gave her a kiss as she left, then returned to the table with Chaz and Danny.

54

Danny, Chaz and Fergus moved through the private jet centre at London's city airport. All three outwardly calm, dressed in Jeans, boots and warm jackets, each with an old arm kitbag on their backs. They passed them through the baggage scanner with no problems and sat in the plush departure lounge. Danny tried Nikki's mobile for the fourth time, hearing it click on to answerphone for the fourth time. He thought about leaving a message, but like the other three times, he couldn't find the words. Flicking through the contacts, he called Scott.

'Daniel, are you alright old chap?' Said Scott, obviously aware something was wrong between him and his sister.

'Is Nikki there Scott?'

'No, I'm afraid not. She's on her way back to Australia. Her flight left at seven this morning. What's going on? All she said was she couldn't sit around waiting to see if you came back.'

'Sorry Scott, I can't really go into it. It's to do with Smudge,' Danny said, seeing one of the airport staff coming to show them to the plane.

'You're going after the man who killed him, aren't you?' Scott said, knowing his best friend too well.

'I'll see you soon,' Danny said, hanging up.

They walked across the tarmac and boarded a waiting Dassault Falcon 8X long range jet. The interior was all shiny and plush, with two rows of large white leather seats facing each other on either side of a highly polished fold-out table. The pilot and copilot greeted them before returning to the cockpit, leaving the stewardess to show them to their seats.

'Whoa, I could get used to this,' Fergus said, letting out a whistle.

'Make yourselves comfortable gentlemen. We have a fully stocked drinks bar and a generous selection of food on board. So once we're in the air, just give me a shout and I'll be happy to serve you.'

They settled in for the nine-hour flight, the tatty old kit bags looking out-of-place sitting on the spare, plush, white leather seats. During the flight, they ran through plans, the satellite pictures and maps spread across the tables. Danny figured they had paid the crew well for their discretion, as the stewardess neither glanced nor blinked an eye at the documents on the table, with their arrows and strategic points marked out in red pen. She just served them food and drinks as they requested, then took her seat at the rear of the plane.

'It's going to be tight,' Fergus said, looking at the satellite image of the house within the compound wall.

'Yeah, fucking ironic that the mission to avenge Smudge's death really needs a four-man team,' Chaz said, sitting back in the chair.

'There's still time for you two to pull out,' Danny said, his face still serious.

'What? And leave you to go in alone. Nah, you're bloody useless without us. You'd get your bollocks shot off inside of five minutes,' Fergus said, smiling.

'Yeah, and I'm coming because you're both useless, and someone's got to pick both of your bollocks up when you get them shot off,' Chaz said, chuckling.

'Great, I feel so much better now,' Danny said, giving in to the banter.

The plane eventually descended, landing smoothly on the tarmac at Wajir Airport. They departed with their bags, walking down the steps into a wall of hot African air. The real possibility that they might not make it back to the plane by 1p.m. on Wednesday, or make it back at all, weighing heavily on their minds. Wajir's terminal building was a small single story affair. They moved swiftly through passport control, the lone officer at his desk looking moderately disinterested as he checked them through. Danny stepped out of the terminal building to find nothing other than an approach road, red soil, and dry scrub land spreading away into the distance, with spaced out trees and twiggy bushes and assorted houses dotted here and there.

'Ok, so where's this guy? What's his name?' Fergus

said, wiping the sweat from his brow.

'His name's Haji. Hang on, I've got a number for him,' Danny said, looking at the paper with his number on.

'Don't bother, I think I've found him,' said Chaz, watching a beaten up old white Mercedes with a Taxi sign on the roof approaching.

They put their hands up to shield their eyes from the setting sun to see the driver grinning as he flashed his lights and waved enthusiastically out the window.

'Subtle little chap, isn't he,' Danny said, picking up his bag.

The taxi pulled up beside them, its brakes screeching loudly as it did so.

'Mr Pearson Sir,' Haji said, grinning as he hopped out of the car to open the boot for their bags.

'How did you guess?' said Danny dryly.

'Are you shitting me? Three white guys in Wajir. Come, get in. We've got a long way to go,' Haji said, beaming even wider.

'In this?' said Chaz, pulling the creaky door open.

'Only to the border. We change vehicles there. Nobody takes any notice of an old taxi,' said Haji, spinning the car around and heading off, the hot air blasting in through the open windows.

'Haji, you've got the equipment we requested?' Danny said.

'Yes Boss, at the other car, two-hour drive, ok.'

Danny nodded across at him and settled into the seat as the old taxi bounced and swerved pot holes along the dirt road, leaving a cloud of fine red dust behind it.

55

A sweaty two hours later, they pulled off the dirt road and stopped, the dim headlights illuminating a ramshackle farm building. Haji got out and pulled open the doors to reveal a Toyota Land Cruiser hand painted a dark green. He drove it out into the open before driving the taxi inside to take its place. Grinning as he opened the back of the Land Cruiser, Haji pulled a tarpaulin back to reveal a pile of weapons, ammunition, armoured vests and radios stacked in front of bottles of water and bags of food and snacks. Danny, Chaz and Fergus moved in to inspect them under the light in the boot.

'What the fuck are these?' said Chaz, picking up an old, scratched, beige and green camouflage painted AR15 rifle.

'They've got to be ten years old. Do they even fire?' Fergus chipped in.

'Hey, look where we are, guys. You think this shit is easy to come across at short notice? Trust me, they're good. Go ahead, try them. There's no one around here for miles.'

Fergus snapped in a magazine then turned and looked through the scope, placing the aim at a tree twenty metres away. He let off a couple of rounds and hit the trunk dead centre.

Danny and Chaz did the same, firing off a few rounds until they were satisfied. They stowed the rifles back in the boot before checking out the SIG Sauer M17 handguns, tatty body armour vests, ammunition, grenades and blocks of C4 with radio detonators.

Finally Chaz took out a Barrett M82 sniper rifle. He loaded a round into it and lay on the floor, folding out the support legs before tucking the stock into his shoulder. He focussed on the furthest tree trunk he could see in the moonlight, slowed his breathing and looked down the scope before squeezing the round gently away. The bullet blew the bark off the tree and embedded itself in the centre of the trunk.

'Ok, we're good, Haji, we'll just get changed before we leave,' Danny said, grabbing his bag and pulling out fatigues bought from an army surplus store to match the jihadi uniform as closely as possible.

'Good, put these around your heads, can't have anyone see those pasty white faces when we get across the border,' said Haji, throwing a black shemagh headscarf to each of them so they could wrap them around their heads and faces, leaving only their eyes on display.

They dressed and kitted up, filling the body armour vests with loaded magazines for the rifles and handguns, hooking on the shared out frag and flash-bang grenades. Chaz took the C4 and radio detonators as he was the explosives expert. Once done, they put their clothes in the kitbags and left them in the taxi, ready to change into on the return journey.

'Haji, how long until we get there?' Danny said as the Land Cruiser bounced along a dirt track that could barely be described as a road.

'About another two hours. Slow going, yes? This is an old sugar smuggling route, they don't use it anymore, not since the Kenyan police shut it down. It's too dangerous to use the main road in—jihadi patrols and roadblocks.'

'Sugar smuggling?' Chaz said.

'Yes, they bring it in at the southern port of Kismayu and run it across Kenya's border, the money goes to fund the jihadi with weapons.'

'Yeah and line the Wolf's pockets,' Chaz grumbled from the back.

They trundled on for what seemed like a hot sweaty age, moving at a crawl several times as Haji turned the lights off and manoeuvred around small collections of whitewashed houses that passed as villages in this remote part of Somalia.

'Fafahdun,' Haji said, turning the headlights off again and pointing towards a group of twinkling lights in the distance.

'Where's the house?' Danny asked.

'It's on the far side of the town, but it's far too dangerous to drive through it. The land dips into a riverbed over to the east with plenty of trees and bushes for cover. It's still dry. We can drive up past the village and get close to the house.'

Danny nodded and Haji drove the Land Cruiser away from the lights of the town, navigating by the moonlight until the land became greener, causing them to weave around trees and bushes as they drove down an incline, eventually bottoming out in the dried-up riverbed. Haji drove at a crawl for another twenty minutes with the headlights off, keeping the revs and noise to an absolute minimum. He turned off the riverbed by a big boulder and weaved his way up the bank through the trees and bushes, stopping and turning the engine off in a dense patch of trees and vegetation just as the land levelled out.

'Town is over that way,' Haji said, pointing past Danny. 'The house is straight ahead, about two hundred metres, ok?'

'Thanks, Haji,' Danny said, looking at his watch. 'Just over two hours until dawn. Let's do a recce before light, then we can bed down for the day and go in tonight.'

Eager to get on with it and even more eager to stretch their legs after the long journey, Chaz and Fergus got straight out of the car.

'Come, come, follow me, I show you,' Haji said, following them out of the car.

'No, you stay here, Haji, this isn't your fight,' Danny said, blocking his way.

'You're wrong. Abshir Ibraham's jihadists killed my family because my father spoke out against them. They dragged them into the street and executed them in front of the whole village to make an example of what happens if you stand up against them. This is my country, my fight.'

Danny, Chaz and Fergus stood quietly for a minute. Danny stepped forward and patted Haji on the shoulder.

'Don't just stand there, man, lead the way,' he said, giving Haji a smile.

Haji returned it with an even bigger smile before moving off through the trees and bushes ahead of them.

56

The trees and bushes thinned out to nothing but dry dirt
twenty metres short of a collection of corrugated tin
shacks and shelters for livestock. A mixture of mud and
block walls formed a maze of enclosures between each
shack, with little pieces of land running in all directions.
At half-past three in the morning, there was no one
about. They passed quickly over open ground, following
Haji along a mud wall, their bodies barely visible in the
dark. He led them into a walled animal compound with
a small corrugated steel barn on one side and a brick-
built shed on the other. They moved slowly to a five-foot
high wall on the far side, trying not to startle the
chickens roaming around their feet as they went. The
smell from the barn twenty feet away burned their
noses—the African heat cooking the ammonia from the
goats' piss inside.

'The house is just over this wall,' Haji said, stopping in
a crouch under the far wall, keeping his head below the

top.

Moving up until they could see over the wall through the slits in their black headscarves, Danny, Chaz and Fergus looked across a patch of open ground at the compound wall and target house beyond. A couple of jihadi soldiers leaned against the wall by the gate, smoking, their guns hanging lazily over their shoulders. Another sat half asleep in the watchtower at the front, with one more just visible on the far side of the compound.

Chaz swung the sniper rifle off his shoulder and rested the barrel on top of the wall. He tucked the stock into his shoulder and took a closer look through the scope.

'What have we got, Chaz?' Danny asked, looking through his less powerful rifle scope.

'Two on the gate, one in each tower, er, a couple of guys walking around inside the wall. I think that's it. Oh, hang on, there's someone on the roof, a white guy with his back to me.'

'Is it the Wolf?' Danny said, moving his rifle up to see a smaller image of the man.

'Hard to say. Come on, turn around, you bastard.'

'Is it him? If it is, take him out,' Danny said, willing the man to turn.

'Wait,' Chaz said, slowing his breathing, the crosshairs through the scope just floating a millimetre over the top of the man's head to allow for the bullet's drop over the distance, his finger resting gently on the trigger.

They all instinctively held their breath as the man turned in their direction.

'It's not him, it's the guy from the lake, that slippery fucking Serbian mercenary piece of shit, er, what's his name?' Chaz said, still glued to the scope.

'Luka Hovat, the one who was with the Wolf when they killed Smudge,' Danny said in a low growl.

'Shall I take him out?' Chaz asked.

'No, not worth the risk. It would alert the Wolf, then he'd be gone and they'd all be all over us. We need to get in, get them both and disable their vehicles on the way out,' Danny said, keeping his emotions in check as he scanned the rest of the compound.

'What's that single-storey building in the grounds? There's a fuel tank by it,' said Fergus, looking to the far side of the property.

Chaz lowered and swung the sniper rifle around to take a better look. 'Looks like a barracks building.'

'What's the tank? Oil? Gas?'

'Fue for the vehicles, I can see the hose and filler nozzle, and the cars are parked nearby. Can't tell if it's diesel or petrol.'

'If it's diesel, will it go up?' Danny asked.

'Yeah, the blast from a C4 block will generate more than enough heat to ignite it, and the explosion will cover the surrounding area in burning fuel.'

'That'll take care of the pickups with the .50 calibre gun mounts. It'll keep the soldiers trapped inside the barracks as well,' said Fergus.

'Yeah, but we need to get inside the compound undetected, lay the charge and be ready to storm the house as soon as it goes off. That way we can sweep the house, kill Luka and the Wolf and be out five minutes tops. What we need is a diversion while me and Ferg get over the wall. Chaz, I need you here with the sniper rifle. As soon as the fuel tank blows, you take out the towers and gate, and keep our exit clear.'

'I can do it,' Haji said with a grin.

'Do what?'

'I can give you a diversion, stall the car near the wall, call them over, tell them I've broken down. It also means I'll be there, ready to move when you get out.'

They all looked at Haji for a few seconds.

'It works for me,' said Fergus.

'You're sure? You don't have to do this,' said Danny, the image of Smudge using the same diversion tactic at Anton Kasovish's house only days before he died flashed across his mind.

'I'm sure, and yes, I do have to do this, for my family,' Haji replied, his face falling.

'Ok, good man.'

'Do something for me.'

'What?' Danny said.

'Kill Abshir Ibraham,' said Haji, looking straight into Danny's eyes.

Looking straight back at Haji, Danny nodded. 'Ok, let's get out of here, get some kip and come back after dark.'

The three of them crouched down below the wall and headed back to the car the way they came. They sat on the floor by the car and watched the sun come up, drinking water and eating protein bars and snacks.

Danny took first watch while the others made themselves as comfortable as possible, keeping out of the sun's blistering heat under the shade of the trees. After two hours, Danny tapped Chaz to take over while he got his head down.

Halfway through his shift, Fergus heard voices amongst the sound of bells and goats bleating. He would have woken Danny and Chaz, but with their minds on subconscious alert, they were already awake and belly crawling over to Fergus. Pushing forward through the bushes, they came to a point where they could see a young Somali boy with his father. They walked on by— unaware of the three rifles pointed at them from beneath the bushes—waving their long sticks as they drove the bleating goats down the incline towards one of the few watering holes next to the dried-up riverbed that still had water in it.

Relieved, the three of them backed away, returned to the car and continued the two-hour watch rotation until the sun finally started to dip on the horizon and the oppressive heat of the day dulled to a warm breeze. They drank and ate the rest of the supplies before checking and rechecking the guns, explosives, and radios. They needn't have checked them again, but the routine action helped keep the nerves in check and pass the hours. At 2 a.m they started to move.

57

Danny, Chaz and Fergus crossed the open ground to the mud wall as they'd done the previous night. Moving along, they entered the animal compound, dodging chickens as they made their way to the far wall. With just their eyes showing through the black headscarves, they checked the target. Two on the gate, one in each watchtower, two patrolling inside the wall, everything as it was last night.

Bobbing back down behind the wall, the three of them moved over to the brick-built shed. Chaz leaned his sniper rifle and his AR-15 against the little building and stepped back. Danny and Fergus put their backs against the shed, bent their knees, and linked their fingers. Chaz placed his boot into Fergus's hands first, then the other one into Danny's. They lifted him slowly, giving him a chance to spread his weight as he rolled onto the corrugated tin roof. It creaked and groaned a little, sounding louder in their heightened state of awareness than it really was. The three of them froze. Chaz lay perfectly still, watching the guards some forty metres away. They didn't move, and no alarm was raised. Chaz beckoned with his hand and Danny passed up the AR-15 rifle. Chaz took it and laid it by his side and beckoned again. Fergus passed up the large Barrett sniper rifle. Chaz took it, folded down the support legs and tucked the stock into his shoulder, immediately targeting the man in the front watchtower before moving the crosshairs to the men on the gate, then moving to the man in the rear watchtower, committing the moves to memory, ready for when they were needed.

'All good, Chaz?' said Danny softly, the throat mic picking up his voice as clear as day in everyone's earpieces.

'Roger that, ready to rock and roll,' Chaz whispered back.

'Haji, are you in position?' Danny said.

'Yes sir.'

'You know what to do?'

'Yes sir.'

'Good, remember to keep your earpiece and throat mic covered by your headscarf, ok? When the shooting starts, get out of there. We'll meet you at the bottom of the hill.'

'Yes sir, I'm rogering that.'

Danny looked at Fergus, the two of them smiling under their headscarves.

'Good man, wait for our mark, Haji. We're moving into position now.'

Danny and Fergus left Chaz and exited the animal compound. They headed down an alley, working their way along a wall, ending up tucked in behind the corner of a small brick house positioned opposite the far corner of the target and some fifteen metres from the gate.

'Haji, you're good to go,' Danny whispered.

'Ok, I'm going now,' Haji said, the sound of the engine following his voice through the earpiece.

They kept out of sight, relying on Chaz's commentary to mark the time to go.

'Here he comes. One hundred metres. Fifty metres. Twenty-five. Here comes the bunny hop. He's at the far corner and he's killed it. On my mark.'

Danny and Chaz could hear Haji get out and shout something in Somali as he lifted the bonnet on the Land Cruiser. Voices came back in return as Haji grabbed the attention of the guards at the gate.

'Get ready, the guards are heading towards Haji and he's got the watchtowers' attention. Just a little more, that's it, dickheads, take a good look at the engine. Go, go, go,' Chaz said calmly, the crosshairs moving smoothly from one target's head to another.

Danny and Fergus ran across the fifteen metres of open ground, tucking in behind the vehicle parked by the wall. Danny gave Fergus a leg up to see over the compound wall. The coast was clear, so he swung his legs over and dropped into the shadows of the far corner. A few seconds later, Danny dropped silently down beside him.

'We're inside the compound.'

'Roger that,' came Chaz's quiet response.

Looking out from the dark, they could see the two guards that had been patrolling the inside of the wall. They stood on a raised platform at the base of the watchtower, looking over the wall at Haji's theatrical car breakdown. Danny and Fergus moved swiftly across to the fuel tank beside the guard's accommodation hut. Peeling the tape off the back of the block of C4 explosive, Danny stuck it halfway up the side of the tank and flicked the switch to on. He paused for a second before reaching into his vest and pulling out a second block of C4.

'Fuck it,' he whispered, flicking the switch on the second device.

'C4 in place. We're heading into the building to detonate.'

'Roger that,' said Chaz, keeping the crosshairs through his scope firmly on the first target, ready to take him out.

Keeping close to the house, Danny moved towards the entrance to the house, Fergus followed behind him, walking backwards to cover the courtyard to their rear. Danny opened the door at arm's length while Fergus looked in from the other side. The hallway was clear, so they moved silently inside.

'Fire in the hole in three. One, two, three,' Danny said, his thumb on the radio detonator in his hand.

At the same time, an armed guard entered the hall from a side room. His eyes locking on Danny with his thumb on the detonator in his hand. As he raised his rifle, Fergus shot him through the heart as Danny pressed the button. Simultaneously, Chaz put a bullet through a guard's head as he stood by Haji and the Land Cruiser.

The explosion shook the building, the igniting fuel covering the courtyard and pickup trucks in a wave of burning liquid, blocking the guards' way out of their accommodation block. Moving the rifle left a touch, Chaz located and dropped the next guard before he realised the man next to him was dead on the ground.

'You used two blocks of C4, didn't you?' Chaz said calmly into the throat mic, while moving his aim to the guard in the watchtower. He was looking into the courtyard at the fire and listening to the shouts from the guards' accommodation, and hadn't seen the two dead men by Haji.

'Yep,' said Danny, heading up the stairs with Fergus.

'You never listen to me. I specifically said you only need one,' Chaz said, squeezing the trigger gently to watch the guard's head explode like a watermelon in the watchtower a fraction of a second later.

'It worked, didn't it?' came Danny's voice over the sound of automatic fire.

'Hostile down,' came Fergus's voice in between their conversation.

'Mmm, I suppose so. Now move yourselves. Haji, get your arse down the hill and keep the engine running. We might be coming in hot.'

'Rogering that, sir,' came Haji's voice.

58

Standing on either side of a heavy hardwood bedroom door, Danny nodded to Fergus before reaching across for the doorknob, keeping his body flat against the wall as he twisted and pushed the door inward. A hail of bullets ripped through the opening, some gouging their way into the hardwood door, others crossing the hallway before blasting plaster off the wall opposite, filling the air with dust and wood splinters.

'Frag,' Fergus said.

'Do it,' Danny replied over another burst of fire ripping through the doorway.

Fergus took a frag grenade off his vest and pulled the pin before flicking his hand around the doorway, throwing the grenade into the centre of the room. They both folded away from the doorway, hands over ears just before the deafening explosion, the blast wave shaking the wall at their backs.

Fergus swung into the room first, spotting Abshir

Ibraham's body on the bed, the white sheets streaked with blood from a shrapnel wound in his chest. A woman lay on her front on the floor by the bed. She shrieked and shouted. As Fergus moved to see if he could help her, she suddenly flipped herself over, revealing an AK-47. Screamed something in Somali, she levelled the rifle in his direction. A spot appeared in the centre of her forehead, followed by the back of her head exploding all over the floor behind her. Fergus turned to see Danny swinging his smoking rifle away and heading back out of the room.

'Ibraham's down, continuing sweep.'

'Roger that,' said Chaz, taking out the guard in the far watchtower.

'I can hear footsteps going for the roof terrace. I'm going up. Have you got eyes on Chaz?' said Fergus, moving up the stairs.

'Not yet,' said Chaz, repositioning.

'Checking the last room, I'll be right behind you,' said Danny, entering a large bedroom at the back of the house.

It looked empty, lit by the dancing orange glow from the burning fuel outside in the courtyard. As Danny moved towards the bathroom, the hand-carved hardwood doors to a built-in wardrobe burst open. Luka grabbed the barrel of Danny's rifle, pushing it to one side with one hand as he brought a SIG Sauer P365 handgun in for the kill shot. Danny instinctively released the grip on his rifle, grabbed and twisted Luka's gun out of his hand with one hand, while punching him in the throat with the other. The rifle and Luka's handgun clattered to the floor. Danny went for his own handgun. Coughing, but still focused, Luka was on him before he got it clear of the holster. Grabbing Danny's vest to bring his knee up into Danny's groin, winding him as he came in for a headbutt. Moving his head to one side, Danny avoided the full impact of Luka's forehead as it grazed painfully off his cheek instead of breaking his nose.

Winded and dizzy, with his handgun rattling to the floor to join the other weapons, Danny stood a couple of metres apart from Luka, breathing heavily, his eyes flicking between the nearest weapons on the floor and Luka's murderous gaze. Reaching behind him, Luka drew his father's ornate hunting knife from its sheath on the back of his belt. Watching the knife's orange glint from the fire's light outside, Danny unwound the headscarf, spinning it tight around his wrists and snapping it tightly like a piece of rope between his hands.

'I have a visual, a woman in a dress and hijab, and a white male. Wait, I can't see his face. It's him, I repeat, it is the Wolf,' said Chaz over the earpiece.

'Take the shot!' Danny shouted as Luka lunged at him.

Twisting to one side, Danny avoided Luka's stab and spun the headscarf around his wrist, snapping his hands apart to grip Luka's wrist tighter, pulling Luka's arm to one side like he was a puppet on a string.

'Negative, he's using the woman as a shield. I don't

have the shot.'

'Keep on him, Chaz, I've got eyes on. He's heading for the steps to the courtyard,' said Fergus, running across the roof terrace in pursuit.

Luka came at Danny with his free hand, powering a fist towards the temple. Already ahead of him, Danny pulled the scarf and Luka's knife hand up, dodging the punch and spinning the rest of the scarf around Luka's other wrist, pulling the material tight to trap both of Luka's wrists together. Gripping both ends of the scarf in the one fist, Danny held Luka's arms down in one hand, leaving him free to punch Luca in the side of the head over and over again. Dazed and punch drunk, Luka struggled to stay upright. Danny suddenly let go and kicked Luka away as hard as he could, then dived to the floor behind the bed. Luka landed on his backside, shaking the scarf free of his wrists as his head cleared. He looked down, taking a second to register the frag grenade hooked into his trouser belt. Knowing his fate, he looked in Danny's direction with hate-filled eyes as the grenade went off, blowing him in half and taking the window out behind him.

Danny picked up his handgun and rifle. He glanced at the pulped remains of Luka before heading down the stairs.

'Luka's down. I'm heading to the courtyard to head off the Wolf.'

'Roger that, I've lost visual,' said Chaz as the Wolf headed down the stairs, facing away from Chaz's view.

'I'm on him,' Fergus said, ducking away from the top

of the stairs as the Wolf fired at him from behind his human shield.

'Klaus Meyer.'

The Wolf turned his head at the shout of his real name, a puzzled look locked on his face. Danny looked back at him from behind his handgun.

'You're not fucking smiling now, are you,' Danny muttered, pulling the trigger, sending a bullet into the centre of the Wolf's forehead.

He stayed upright on the stairs for a second or two, his body taking a moment to figure out his brain wasn't controlling it. Finally, his arms fell away from his human shield and his legs buckled. His body tumbled down the stairs, finishing up at Danny's feet.

'That's for Smudge,' Danny said, looking down at him. 'Let's go, Ferg.'

Fergus hurried past the shocked woman sobbing through the hijab that covered all but her eyes.

'Get your arses out of there. The guards are coming out of the accommodation block,' Chaz said urgently.

Danny looked over to the far side of the courtyard to see the pickup trucks still burning, but the burning fuel surrounding the accommodation block was dwindling and the guards started running through it, guns ready, eager to know who was attacking them.

'Get to the wall under the watchtower, now,' Chaz shouted, his voice a little shaky as he abandoned the large sniper rifle, grabbed his AR-15 and jumped down off the brick shed, running across the open ground to the compound wall as fast as his legs would carry him.

'Roger that.'

59

The guards didn't react to Fergus with the same head-covering and close enough uniform. He looked like one of them as he ran around the side of the house in the dark, heading for the watchtower. The situation exploded when Danny followed, his head exposed, a white armed westerner, standing out like Batman at a Spiderman convention. Bullets blasted masonry off the surrounding walls, whizzing past his head as he rounded the building.

'Whatever you're doing, Chaz, do it quickly,' Danny said, powering after Fergus, shouts and gunfire echoing not far behind him.

'Fire in the hole,' Chaz said a couple of seconds before an explosion lit up the outside of the wall in front of them.

Concrete block and render flew all over the place, the dust clearing ahead of them to expose a six-foot-wide section of the wall missing, with Chaz resting his rifle on the jagged brickwork to one side as he aimed his rifle and fired short bursts at the guards giving chase. He dropped two before the others ducked back out of sight. Fergus jumped through the hole in the wall and immediately turned to take his place on the opposite side of the hole to Chaz, rifle up, covering Danny as he sprinted the last few metres and jumped through the gap between them.

'Haji, I hope you're ready, mate. We're coming in hot,' Danny said, keeping tight to the wall as he ran down the hill. He stopped twenty metres down, leaning against the wall with his rifle up, covering Chaz and Fergus as they ran past him towards the car.

'Don't worry, boss, Haji is coming.'

Counting ten seconds in his head, Danny turned and continued down the hill, knowing Fergus or Chaz were covering him from further down. Looking ahead, Fergus had tucked in behind a corrugated shack, aiming up the road behind him. Chaz continued running down the hill. Not far ahead, Danny saw the reversing lights of the Land Cruiser, its engine whining as Haji reversed it flat out up the hill, sliding to a halt just in front of Chaz, who pulled the rear door open for Danny before jumping in the front passenger seat. Danny turned at the car, dropping to one knee to steady his rifle against his deep breathing. He looked past Fergus to the hole in the wall beyond, firing two short bursts at the jihadi soldiers looking through the hole in the wall. He didn't hit them, but the bullets ricocheted off the wall close enough to send them back inside. Fergus reached the car and dived in through the open door, sliding across the seat to make room for Danny as he got in and slammed the door shut.

'Go, go, go,' Chaz said in the front.

Haji floored it down the hill while Danny and Fergus twisted in their seats and watched for anyone following.

'Haji, what's the fastest you can get us across the border?' Danny said.

'If we take the main road, we can go much faster, maybe forty minutes. We can cut across to the smugglers' route a couple of miles before the border checkpoint. But it's dangerous. We might come across a patrol or roadblock.'

'Do it, and make it thirty minutes. Any second now, that lot's going to find out we've killed their leader and go nuts.'

Haji took Danny's request to heart and accelerated dangerously through the town. Lights came on and nervous faces dared to peep out from the shacks, awakened and scared by all the gunfire and explosions. Haji didn't touch the brakes as they left the town, sliding the Land Cruiser sideways in a cloud of dust as he bumped up onto the tarmac of the main road.

Back at the house, the guards had discovered Abshir Ibraham's body and were running around shouting and firing guns into the air in rage. They crammed into the two 4x4s outside the wall, driving off through the town in pursuit of the Land Cruiser, arms out of the windows, banging on the outside of the cars to make the drivers go faster.

60

After staring out the rear window for several minutes, Danny and Chaz looked at each other.

'They're gaining,' Chaz said, his eyes flicking back to the hazy headlights barely visible through the dust cloud kicked up by the Land Cruiser.

'Haji, can you get any more speed out of this tub of crap?' Danny said, turning his head to the front.

'I don't know, the engine's getting very hot.'

'It's going to get a hell of a lot hotter in here if we don't speed up,' Danny said, turning back to watch the closing headlights.

'Ok boss,' Haji said, pushing the accelerator the small distance left to flatten it to the floor.

'What do you think?' Chaz said.

Danny looked at his watch, then back out the rear window at the headlights in the distance. 'I think we're pulling away. If we can keep going like this until we turn off, Haji can turn the lights off and whisk us away down the smugglers' route into Kenya.'

'How much longer?'

'Fifteen minutes, give or take a couple.'

'How are we doing back there?' said Fergus from the front.

'Peachy, mate. Me and Danny were just thinking about buying some property out here, what with the sunny climate and friendly locals,' said Chaz with a chuckle.

'If you think this lot are hostile, you want to try living with Gaynor, she'd eat that lot of pussies for breakfast,' said Fergus, managing a smile despite the tension in the car.

'I'm starting to think we should have brought her with us,' said Danny.

After a shared grin, the car fell into a tense silence. Five minutes went by, then ten. The headlights faded to faint specks, visible then not visible as the 4x4s rose and dipped on the undulating road behind them.

With the turnoff to join the smugglers' route only a few miles ahead, the engine made a loud bang before rattling on like someone had emptied a bag of bolts into it. If it hadn't been so dark they would have seen the clouds of diesel smoke billowing out of the exhaust.

'I think we're in trouble,' said Haji, changing down the gears to keep the Land Cruiser going as the engine lost power.

Danny looked around, his eyes fixing on a collection of lights and silhouetted buildings a mile or so off from the road. 'Haji, kill the lights and head for the village.'

Haji immediately clicked the lights off and turned the ever slowing car off the tarmac, crawling and bouncing along the dirt track, rolling past the first few houses as the engine died. Danny and Chaz were out first, down on one knee, rifles up with eyes glued to the sights, watching the headlights growing larger on the main road.

'Ferg, you and Haji push the car out of sight.'

'Roger that,' Fergus said, pointing behind the nearest house to Haji.

Danny and Chaz's rifles moved smoothly in unison, tracking the jihadis' 4x4s as they approached the turnoff for the village. They held their breath, finally giving a sigh of relief as the two vehicles sped past the turnoff and continued their chase along the main road.

'How far to the border?' Danny said, turning to Haji as he appeared from behind the house with Fergus.

'Er, about five kilometres to the border and another two to the taxi.'

Danny looked around the village as best as he could in the dark. 'Let's find a vehicle, any vehicle.'

'Er, guys,' Chaz said from behind them.

'You still remember how to hot-wire a car?' Danny said to Fergus, not listening to Chaz.

'Easy, mate, it's like riding a bike,' Fergus said with a grin.

'Danny,' Chaz said more urgently.

'Ok, take Haji with you and get a vehicle. What is it, Chaz?' Danny said, turning to see Chaz still on one knee, his eye still glued to the sight.

'They didn't buy it,' Chaz said, watching the vehicles stop a couple of miles down the main road before turning and heading back towards the dirt track to the village.

'Ferg, make it quick, we've got incoming.'

'Roger that,' Fergus said, already several houses away, looking for a vehicle, any vehicle.

'I'll take left, you take right, take them out in a kill box as soon as they enter the village,' Danny said, crossing the dirt road to position himself behind the corner of a mud built shack.

'Roger that,' Chaz said, standing up slowly, his eye still looking down the rifle sight at the vehicles as they bounced off the main road a mile away and headed towards them. 'Here they come.'

'How much ammo have you got?'

'Three full. One in the rifle, two in the vest, and two spare for the SIG.'

'Grenades?' Danny added.

'One frag, what about you?' Chaz said, still calmly watching the approaching vehicles around the corner of a wall.

'Fifteen in the rifle plus two full mags, two spare for the SIG, no grenades.'

'So what's the plan?' Chaz said.

'Quick burst, half a mag each to take out the lead vehicle, then you throw the frag grenade at the rear vehicle while I give cover. You good with that?'

'Well, it's a plan. I'll go on your mark,' said Chaz, outwardly calm while the adrenaline levels were rising inside.

'Good, because it's the only plan I've got,' Danny whispered over the throat mic.

They tucked in tighter behind the corners as the headlights got close enough to light up the road and houses in front of them, changing the ground from monochrome greys to shades of red and brown.

The engine noise dropped to a tick-over, and they heard the occupants yelling at each other. A few seconds later the lead vehicle continued to move towards them while the jihadis got out of the vehicle behind and entered the village on foot.

'Shit, no time to plan. We'll hit the lead vehicle and wing it,' Danny said.

'Roger that,' Chaz replied.

'Ok, a little closer, closer, closer. Mark.'

61

Danny squeezed off three bullets tightly grouped at the front passenger from his position on the left. At the same time, Chaz targeted the driver. Both men died instantly, leaving the vehicle rolling forwards. The rear doors burst open as the remaining jihadis jumped out of the car, yelling and firing wildly. Breathing calmly, Danny tracked the first man, double-tapping him as bullets blew bits of brick and mud off the side of the house in front of him. Chaz took out the two men as they exited his side, leaving two more sliding out of the back door, crouching behind the car for cover.

Back at the 4x4 parked at the edge of the village, the jihadi soldiers ran to either side of the road before working their way between the houses, heading towards Danny and Chaz, firing off potshots as they advanced.

'Ferg. We could really do with a vehicle out of here, like now mate,' said Danny, sliding in a fresh magazine.

'There are no fucking vehicles. Just hold tight. I've got

an idea.'

'Whatever it is, do it quickly,' Danny replied between shots.

'Fuck this,' said Chaz. Pulling the last frag grenade off his vest. He pulled the pin and threw it low, bouncing it off the mud like skimming a stone on water, until it rolled to a stop under the vehicle ten metres away from them.

It exploded under the fuel tank a few seconds later, ripping through the bottom of the vehicle, engulfing it and the two jihadi soldiers behind in a massive fireball.

'How many do you make it, six?' Chaz said.

'Five,' Danny said, putting a man down as he crossed from one building to another.

'Ferg? Where the fuck are you?'

'Be with you in thirty seconds,' came Fergus's slightly out of breath reply.

Chaz took another man out before changing the magazine. They heard shots over the earpiece, and a revving engine that coincided with the lights of the jihadis' 4x4 coming on at the edge of the village. It accelerated down the street as Fergus fired out of the window, killing the unexpecting soldiers as they moved on Danny. Haji drove with one arm out the window as he fired Fergus's SIG handgun, killing the last two soldiers as they moved towards Chaz. Continuing forward, Haji squeezed around the burning vehicle and slid to a halt between Danny and Chaz.

'What are you waiting for, a number ten bus? Hurry up and get in,' Fergus shouted with a big grin on his face.

Danny and Chaz didn't need telling twice, barely having time to pull the doors shut before Haji gunned the vehicle through the village and out the back end, leaving a trail of dust behind them. When they were well clear, Haji slowed and headed out into the wilderness, eventually picking up the smugglers' trail towards the border.

They crossed into Kenya as the sky on the horizon turned from black to red and blue, pulling up at the ramshackle farm building as the sun appeared above the horizon. The three of them changed and checked phones and passports, while Haji pulled the taxi out. They threw all the clothes, weapons, and vests into the 4x4, while Haji fetched a petrol can out of the farm building, emptying it all over the interior of the vehicle before flicking a match inside. They watched it go up in flames without saying a word, then got in the taxi and headed off on the bumpy road towards the airport. Now they were safely in Kenya, and with the adrenaline of the previous night long gone, Danny, Fergus, and Chaz slept as Haji drove on.

'Hey, sirs, we are here,' Haji said, pulling to a halt outside the small terminal building.

Getting out, they yawned and stretched as Haji got their near empty kitbags out of the boot.

'Thanks, Haji, we couldn't have done it without you,' Danny said, moving in to give the little man a hug and slap on the back.

'Yeah, you're a legend, mate,' said Fergus, taking over

with a hug.

'If you're ever in Blighty, you look us up,' Chaz said, shaking Haji's hand before bringing him in for another hug and slap on the back.

'Thank you, sirs, I won't forget you. My family is now avenged and Abshir Ibraham will rot in Jahannam,' Haji said, his face turning melancholy before returning to a grin as he waved goodbye and climbed back into the taxi.

They watched him go, then entered the small terminal building, passing the same disinterested officer on the passport control desk to sit in the boiling hot waiting room used for departures. At ten past twelve the private jet came in to land. They waited for a tanker to refuel it before walking across the hot tarmac and boarding. A few minutes before 1 p.m the stewardess pulled the door shut, they buckled up, sat back and listened to the engine roar as the plane took off.

'Good afternoon, gentlemen. I hope your trip was a good one. Would you like a drink, something to eat?' The stewardess said once they were at cruising altitude.

'Just a coffee for me, please,' Danny said, tiredness, sombre reflection and thoughts of their missing comrade spinning around in his head, along with the yearning to see Nikki.

Chaz and Fergus were feeling the same. After refreshments, they sat in silence, individually locked in their thoughts. The three of them slept for the rest of the flight. The pilot's announcement waking them up as they came into land at London's City Airport.

'Just one more thing to do then,' said Fergus, looking out the windows at London's lights twinkling below him in the night.

'Yep, tomorrow at 11 a.m ok?' said Chaz.

'Yeah 11's fine,' said Danny, putting the seat upright to land.

They went their separate ways when they exited the terminal. Danny hopped in a cab and made it through his front door just before midnight. He dropped his bag and walked into the kitchen. The house felt cold and empty.

62

At 10:55 a.m, Danny walked through the gated arch of the City of London Cemetery. The weather was cold, dull and overcast, but at least it was dry. He made his way through the rows of gravestones, some large, some small, some huge monuments to loved ones passed. He found Chaz and Fergus standing by a fresh grave, the soil still raised, yet to settle and sink to a slight mound. A small wooden cross was at its head. The marble headstone they'd paid for wouldn't be placed until the ground had settled and gone hard. They stood at the foot of the grave. Fergus reached into his carrier bag and brought out a four-pack of beers. He pulled one off and placed it by the cross before passing one to Danny and Chaz. The three of them cracked the lids, raised the cans to Smudge's grave, and took a drink.

'Here's to you, Smudge. We're going to miss you, mate,' said Chaz.

'Sleep well, brother,' said Fergus.

'I'm going to miss you, you dopey bastard,' Danny said, taking another swig.

'Right, I'm off. You want a lift, Ferg?' Chaz said.

'Yeah, thanks, Chaz.'

'Danny?'

'No, you two go on. I'm going to stick around for a while,' Danny said, looking over to another area of the graveyard he knew only too well.

'Ok, we'll catch you later, mate,' Chaz said, knowing where Danny was going.

When they were gone, Danny visited his mother's grave, standing for a while before moving to the graves of his wife and son, reading the inscriptions as he always did.

"Sarah Ann Pearson, Beloved Wife and Mother, I'll Love You Forever."

"Timothy Robert Pearson, Beloved Son, I'll Never Forget."

He heard footsteps as he looked at the headstones, the sound of the expensive leather-soled handmade shoes, familiar as they approached and stopped beside him.

'I hear you had a productive trip. The powers that be are most pleased,' said Simon in his usual upbeat manner.

'I can't tell you how happy I am to hear that,' Danny replied sarcastically.

'Now, now, Mr Pearson, one should never underplay one's achievements.'

'That's enough kissing my arse. What do you want, Simon? I'm kind of busy here,' Danny said gruffly.

'Fair enough. There's a situation brewing. A situation that could use a man of your talents. A situation that I'm authorised to pay very handsomely to get resolved.'

'We're done Simon, all dues paid. I'm out for good,' Danny said, looking him squarely in the eyes.

Simon just smiled and gave a curt nod before turning. 'We'll see Mr Pearson. Take care of yourself,' he said, walking away.

63

An hour later, Simon walked briskly through Hyde Park, following the path that ran alongside the lake. Moving to a bench near the top end, Simon sat down next to a middle-aged man in a suit, his face buried behind a copy of the Financial Times. He brushed a bit of lint off his trousers as he crossed his legs and gazed across the lake at the Princess Diana Memorial Garden.

'Good afternoon, Simon. The committee is extremely impressed with the way your man dealt with our little problem,' the man said, folding the paper with purposeful exactness before placing it on his lap.

'Thank you, General. You know, the situation could have been resolved a lot quicker if you'd come to me before the attack on the farmhouse,' Simon said, with no emotional inflection.

'A lag in the chain of information, my dear fellow. Our department deals in the UK's secure future by exerting influences on foreign shores. What happens closer to home is your department.'

'Very true, it's just a shame we didn't know sooner that Meyer, the Wolf, Benedict, or however you want to refer to him, was one of yours,' Simon said, checking his polished shoes were immaculately clean.

'The Wolf? No, he wasn't ours. Arthur Montgomery was our man. We found Klaus Meyer when he stole Vincent Benedict's identity. He was just a small-time crook. Drugs, small arms deals and ideas of grandeur. It was Montgomery's job to move him into the big time. We invented an MOD contact for Montgomery to facilitate the Wolf's dealings and supplied Montgomery with the client list.'

'So what went wrong?'

'Montgomery went rogue. He started mixing in high circles, introducing the Wolf to politicians, secretly securing new weapons suppliers from the money coming from the drug deals. If it hadn't been for David Wallace's pictures and notebook forcing them to show their hand, we'd still be in the dark. He had to go,' the General said, looking at his watch.

'You killed Montgomery?'

'Are you going to use Pearson for the job in Istanbul?' the General said, ignoring Simon's question with a smile.

'No, I'm afraid he is unavailable for the time being. I've got someone else in mind for that.'

'What a shame. Don't let him vacate for too long. He's far too great an asset to lose.'

'He'll be back General, I can assure you of that,'

Simon said with absolute confidence.

'Glad to hear it. He still has no idea he was part of the Jerico experiment?' The General said.

'No, he does not. Nor does he know the only other successful candidate is still alive.'

'Nicholas Snipe's success is still up for debate, especially after he went criminally insane and nearly ruined the western world's economy over that Marcus Tenby affair. I'm still under the opinion you should have let him die.'

'As far as Pearson is concerned, he killed Snipe in the attack on the gym. The facility has done an amazing job since he came out of the coma. Snipe has no recollection of his and Mr Pearson's altercation, and has completed three successful assignments without issue. In fact, it's Snipe who's going to Istanbul.'

'Well, it's your call, Simon. You know my feelings on the subject. Anyway, it's time to go,' the General said, standing up.

'Goodbye, General. A pleasure doing business with you, as always,' Simon said, shaking his hand.

'Goodbye Simon.'

The two men left the bench, walking in opposite directions, seemingly unconnected to all around them.

64

Looking out of her front window at the for sale sign, Nikki wondered if she should take it off the market. She hadn't heard anything from Danny since she left London, and didn't know where he was. Her phone ringing pulled her away from the window. Wiping a tear from her eye, she went into the kitchen and picked up the mobile.

'Hi sis, how are you?' said her brother Scott.

Her resolve broke down, and she sobbed down the phone. 'Where is he? I called and left messages. He's not answered any of them.'

'Don't cry, sis. He's back. I spoke to him yesterday,' Scott said gently.

'He's back, and he's ok? What did he say?'

'Not much really. He turned up at my apartment, gave me his keys, and asked if I could look after his house for a while. He said he had something important he had to do and left.'

'That's it, nothing else?' Nikki said, pulling herself together and wiping the tears from her eyes.

'No, sorry sis, that's all he said. Just give him a little time. I'm sure he'll contact you.'

'I don't know anymore. You think so?'

'Absolutely, my dear. He's crazy about you.'

There was an awkward silence as Nikki tried to convince herself everything would be alright.

'Anyway, that's not why I'm calling. I've been offered a rather lucrative contract from a Brazilian company. They're flying me out next week, five-star hotel, all expenses paid. I agreed under the condition they pay for my PA as well. The PA would be you, sis. I thought you might like a little break away from it all. I'll pay for your flight from Australia.'

'Oh, Scott, that's a lovely idea, but with all this going on with Danny, I don't know.' The front doorbell rang before Scott replied. 'Hang on, Scott, there's somebody at the door,' she said, putting the phone down on the kitchen table to answer it. She opened the door to find Danny standing there. She opened her mouth to speak, but he silenced her.

'Wait, just listen,' he said, his eyes looking into hers, dark, soft, and kind. 'Look, I'm sorry I went off. It's over now, all of it. Revenge for Smudge, the stuff with Simon, everything. All I want is you, here, in the UK, anywhere.'

With that, Danny went down on one knee and pulled a little blue box out of his pocket.

'Nikki Miller, will you marry me?' Danny said,

opening the box to show her a diamond engagement ring.

Nikki's mouth dropped open and tears welled up in her eyes. 'Yes, I will.'

Danny stood up and removed the ring from the box. Placing it on her shaking finger. Nikki looked at it, then at him, hugging him before moving slowly back to kiss him. She pulled back and smiled before a frown crossed her face. 'Oh wait, shit, Scott's still on the phone,' she said, grabbing Danny's hand and pulling him inside.

'Scott, you still there?'

'Yes, just about. I thought you'd forgotten about me.'

'You know that trip to Brazil? Can I bring somebody with me?' she said, smiling back at Danny.

'I suppose so, er, who?'

'Danny, he's here, and guess what?' Nikki said, putting the mobile on speakerphone.

'Oh God, I dread to think, do tell,' Scott said, secretly pleased that Danny had turned up.

'We're getting married.'

'What? Married? Are you sure?' Scott said in surprise.

'Thanks for the vote of confidence, Scotty boy,' Danny said, grabbing Nikki and picking her up off her feet.

'Sorry old boy, it was just a bit of a shock, er, my sincerest congratulations.'

'Thanks mate, see you in Brazil,' Danny shouted back from the hallway as he carried Nikki away into the bedroom.

'Er, yes, good, of course. I'll see you in Brazil then.

Danny? Er hello, Nikki? Anyone?'

Please, please, please leave a review for the No Upper Limit

As a self published indie author, I can't stress enough how important your Amazon reviews are to getting my work out there.

I love writing these books for you, it takes months of hard work to create each one. So please take a few minutes to click the book link below, scroll down to reviews and leave a short review or just star rate it.

Thank you so much
Stephen Taylor

Scan to review No Upper Limit

Choose your next Danny Pearson novel
The Danny Pearson books can be read in any order,
But here they are in the order they were written:

Vodka Over London Ice
The London mob clash with the Russian Mafia.
The death and violence escalate, putting Danny's family
in danger.
Danny Pearson has to end the war, before more family
die…

Execution of Faith
Terrorists and mercenary killers plot to change the
balance of world power.
Can Danny Pearson stop them or will this be his
downfall...

Who Holds The Power
As a Secret organisation kills, corrupts and influences its
way to global domination. Danny Pearson must stop
them and their deadly Chinese assassin in his most
dangerous adventure to date...

Alive Until I Die
When government cutbacks threaten project Dragonfly.
General Rufus McManus takes direct action to secure its
future. Deep undercover with his life on the line, can
Danny survive long enough to bring him to justice…

Sport of Kings

When Danny's old SAS buddy goes missing, Danny's
unit reunite to find him. When they follow Smudges trail
they find themselves on the wrong side of an
international drug smuggling operation and the sport of
kings, an exclusive hunt of a deadly nature...

Blood Runs Deep

Five Years Ago (Vodka Over London Ice) The London
mob clashed with the Russian Mafia. Death and
violence escalated, putting Danny's family in danger.
Danny Pearson ended the war, or so he thought...

Command To Kill

When Australian billionaire Theodore Blazer takes
advantage of todays plugged in world with sinister
intentions, Danny travels to the far side of the globe to
stop the world falling apart.

No Upper Limit

Journalist David Wallace is killed when he tries to find
out the identity of an arms dealer known as the Wolf,
Danny Pearson's SAS unit is also trying to stop the Wolf
selling arms to the Taliban. When they get close the
Wolf disappears forever, or so they thought...

Leave Nothing To Chance

When Danny's best friend Scott goes missing from his
hotel room in Brazil, Danny pulls out all the stops to find

him. The search takes him into the heart of Columbia and the clutches of a drugs baron known as El Diablo. **(Coming 2023)**

Available on Amazon

Read on for an extract from
Vodka Over London Ice

ONE

Under a cloud-covered night sky, four figures exited a
Russian-built Mi-8 helicopter into the dry Afghanistan
wasteland. They fanned out, taking a knee, rifles up at
the ready. Their eyes scanned the terrain through night
scopes. The helicopter's engines grew louder, the
increased downdraft peppering their backs with stinging
grit as it left. As soon as the noise died away, the team
leader signalled them onwards. It had dropped them five
miles from their target destination to avoid detection.

They broke into a fast tab to cover the distance.
Checking his GPS, the lead signalled stop. They drank
to rehydrate as streams of sweat ran down their grease-
painted faces. The SAS team lay on their bellies,
peeping over the ridge of a dried-up riverbed. Smudge
focused through his night sight, keeping watch through
the eerie green enhanced view on their target. The
team's leader, Danny Pearson, ran through the intel and
mission plan one last time.

'Ok, guys, intel puts the hostages in this compound
here. Our objective is to get diplomat Richard Mann,
his wife and his son out. If we can do that without things
turning into a shitstorm, all the better,' said Danny,
tapping the aerial reconnaissance photo.

'We'll follow the natural cover of the riverbed to here.
On the all clear, we'll have to sprint the final forty
metres of open ground up to the wall. Ok?' He paused
for the teams' affirmation.

'At the wall, Smudge, Chaz, you cover the alley to
the north and our exit route south. Me and Fergus will
enter the compound here and extract the hostages.'

Their senses heightened as the rising adrenaline
flowed through their veins.

'Remember, if the shit hits the fan, lay down heavy
covering fire and get back here. I'll call in an air strike
and we'll move out for extraction. Ok?'

Following the plan, they moved along the low-lying
riverbed. It wound left and right until it eventually
cornered close to the wall. Heads barely over the bank,
they checked out the compound through their sights.

'Guard two o'clock, top of the east corner,' said Chaz.

'Roger that,' said Danny.

'Guard heading away from us up the northern alley,' said Smudge, scanning the far corner.

'I see him. Roger that.'

They watched for a few more minutes to be sure no more guards were on sentry duty. The drone images in their mission intel showed around a dozen Al Qaeda fighters in the compound.

'Guard on the wall is moving away,' said Chaz, his eyes still glued to the target.

'Ok, get set, we move on three.'

Danny paused for a few more seconds to make sure the guard didn't turn back.

'One, two, three.'

Moving as fast as they could with forty kilos of kit on their backs, the men ran tight and low to the base of the compound wall. Swivelling around they planted their backs against it, guns immediately up as the four of them covered every direction, listening.

Silence. No yelling, no alarm raised.

'Right, let's get this done by the book, guys. No heroics,' said Danny, waving off Smudge and Chaz to cover the far corner while he and Fergus headed for the compound entrance.

Two metres from the corner, Smudge lay down on his front while Chaz took a knee, his back to Smudge as he covered the rear and Danny's exit route. Moving incredibly slowly Smudge edged forward in silence in the dark. He got his eyes around the corner and looked up the northern alley. His eyes searched in the one dim light source from a lamp at the top of the alley. To his surprise a red dot appeared no more than four metres away. A guard's face glowed red as he leaned back against the wall and sucked on his cigarette.

Fighting the urge to flinch away, Smudge inched back behind the corner. He tapped Chaz on the shoulder and signalled eyes on one. Sliding off his pack and rifle he pulled his knife and turned back. Chaz stood glued to the corner, silenced gun at the ready if needed. Smudge moved painstakingly slowly into the darkness of the alley.

Bored and tired, the guard finished his cigarette, throwing the butt to the ground. He reached for his rifle propped up against the wall. He didn't get close. A hand clamped over his mouth, the feeling of cold steel against his hot neck barely having time to register. Smudge thrust the knife up into the base of his skull, killing him instantly.

'Contact. Hostile down. Mission still a go,' came over Danny's earpiece.

'Roger that. Entering compound now.'

Keeping as flat against the wall as he could, Danny crouched by the arched entrance to the compound. Reaching into his pack, he removed a little telescopic rod with a mirror attached. Extending it slowly at floor level, he twisted it around until he finally picked up the reflection of two guards just inside.

'Two. Ten yards in, right-hand side,' he whispered into his throat mic.

'Roger that,' came Fergus's whispered reply.

'I'll take those two, you cover my back and look for the one up on the wall,' whispered Danny, packing the mirror stick away and exchanging it for his suppressed rifle.

'Roger that,' came Fergus's reply, as he tucked in tighter behind Danny.

'On my mark. You all clear, Smudge?'

Lying on top of the dead guard as he covered the alley, Smudge nodded to Chaz.

'Affirmative, good to go.'

Danny swung around through the arch, eyeing the guards. He double-tapped two shots into centre mass of each guard, dropping them like a stone. Another couple of metallic pings sounded behind him, followed by a thud as the guard fell off the wall onto the dirt floor. They took a knee with guns up, covering the courtyard in anticipation of attack. No alarm. No guards. All quiet.

The two of them dragged the bodies behind a beaten-up old pickup truck parked against the compound wall. They continued towards the building that on the satellite pictures was marked as the hostage location.

'Hostiles down. Proceeding to hostage location,' whispered Danny over the mic.

'Roger that. Perimeter clear,' replied Chaz.

They moved low past the first building. Lights were on and they could hear voices chattering and laughing through the open windows. Danny moved in the lead to the door of the hostage block, with Fergus walking backwards, covering the rear.

'I'll take point, you take my left,' whispered Danny as they both stood, ready to storm the building.

'Roger that.'

Moving through the door fast, they fell into a well-practiced search manoeuvre. As they swept through the rooms, they found no guards. The reason became clear as soon as they entered the last room. Lying on the ground three feet away from his own head, was the diplomat's decapitated body. Lying next to him on their sides with their hands tied behind them lay his wife and son with their throats cut, their faces locked in the terrifying last moments of life.

They stood locked, unable to pull away from the scene for a few long seconds. The smell of death and sound of buzzing flies was etching its way into their memories forever.

'Fuck! Fucking bastards,' said Danny, the shock sending his mind spiralling. His own wife and child had been killed a couple of years ago, when a lorry driver crushed their car before driving off, never to be found. Deep suppressed feelings came flooding to the surface as he looked at the bodies in front of him, images of his wife and son appearing over the top of them as his mind overloaded with emotion.

'Fucking bastards. Bastards.'

'Mission abort. Hostages are dead. We're coming out. Prepare for evac,' said Fergus, tapping Danny on the shoulder.

'Roger that,' came Smudge's reply.

'Danny—time to go, mate.'

Dazed, Danny followed Fergus out the door without responding. As they passed the building with the lights on Danny stopped.

'Fucking bastards,' he kept muttering over and over.

'Danny! What you doin', Boss?' asked Fergus, watching horrified as Danny charged the door. Inside the shocked Al Qaeda fighters stumbled and tripped out of their chairs, trying frantically to grab their rifles. A hail of fully automatic fire ripped through the room. Blood and plaster filled the air. None of them managed to get a round off before Danny's gun clicked empty. As the dust settled, the door from the kitchen burst open and a screaming fanatic hurtled towards him with a meat cleaver in his hand. Still enraged beyond reason, Danny dropped his rifle and charged directly at the man, pulling his commando knife from its sheath as he went. A second before contact, the man flew backwards onto a bunk in a cloud of red mist, three rounds from Fergus's rifle hitting him squarely in the chest.

Danny pulled to a stop, breathing heavily with a tear rolling down his cheek. Fergus came up next to him and put his arm around his shoulder.

'Come on, mate, it's over. Let's go home.'

His face hard as granite, Danny wiped his eyes, turned and picked up his rifle. Loading a fresh magazine into it, he walked out of the building.

'Smudge, Chaz, we're coming out. Clear for evac,' he said.

'All clear, Boss, come on out.'

I can't do this anymore—I'm done.

TWO

Harry Knight sat on a kitchen stool, reading his morning paper over the white marble-topped breakfast bar. His wife, Louise, clicked around the kitchen in her high heels. He dressed immaculately as always; this morning's choice a Saville Row charcoal suit and matching waistcoat, snuggly fitted over a crisp white shirt and dark grey silk tie. His platinum submariner Rolex was just visible under shirt cuffs held together with diamond-encrusted gold HK cufflinks.

'Thanks, love,' he said as his wife put a cup on a coaster in front of him.

'Right, I'm off now, Harry. I've got to drop May off at college then I'm meeting the girls for lunch later,' said Louise, kissing him on the cheek as she grabbed her Gucci handbag and keys.

'Ok, love. I've gotta go to the club tonight so I'll be late home,' he shouted after her. He heard an 'Ok' echo back from the hall, followed by her calling for their daughter.

May's face appeared around the door to the lounge, a carefree, happy smile spread widely across it.

'Bye, Dad,' she said.

'Bye, darlin'. Have a good day,' he said softly back.

'Coming!' she shouted, disappearing out the other door.

Harry could hear Louise talking to someone at the front door.

'Harry, Bob's here. Go through, love. He's in the kitchen,' she said, slamming the front door in her hurry to leave.

Bob Angel came in through the kitchen door at an angle; the size of his shoulders wouldn't fit head-on. The ex-bare knuckle fighter was sporting a little middle-age spread these days, but that aside, he still cast a formidable shadow. He was dressed in a dark blue tailored suit. It looked out of place for a man with a flat crooked nose and hands like shovels but Harry insisted all his guys wore smart suits.

'We're businessmen, not street thugs,' he'd say.

'All right, Bob, what brings you here this early? You were at the club til four, weren't you?' said Harry, looking up from his paper. 'You wanna coffee?'

Harry got up and moved around the kitchen to make his oldest friend and right-hand man a drink.

'Yes, please, Boss. I'm round early cause we've had a bit of trouble at the club and down the Dog-n-Duck,' said Bob, the stool creaking under his weight.

Frowning, Harry put the drink down on a coaster in front of Bob. He picked up his own and remained standing.

'Go on,' he said.

'We caught one of Volkov's guys dealing in the club again last night, and Pete's had two of them approach him in the Dog. They threatened him, said he had to use them to supply the booze to the pub, or else,' said Bob, his thick cockney accent remaining calm.

'Viktor fucking Volkov, that cheeky Russian bastard,' said Harry, turning his back to Bob. He looked out the large bi-folding patio doors, thinking. A workman was jet-washing his patio while the gardener inspected his carefully manicured lawn.

'That little prick's been warned about this before and he's still takin' the piss. Get some of the lads together, track down Viktor's scummy little runners and give them a good hidin'—not enough to put 'em in hospital, but hard enough that they don't forget it. Tell them to fuck off back south of the river and stay there,' he said, turning back to Bob and spilling his coffee on the breakfast bar as he put it down.

'Shit, better mop that up. Lou will have my guts for garters.'

Bob chuckled to himself. The great Harry Knight— the man who built an empire of pubs, clubs, betting shops and property any way he could was still not the boss of his own home.

'How's the fight coming along, Bob?' asked Harry, getting back to business.

'Good, Harry, the kid looks mustard. Bets are well up. The other guy's a four-to-one long-shot. He's a good lad, happy with the bung. He'll go down in the third,' said Bob, beaming. He still loved the thrill of the fight game.

'Great. The warehouse all set up ok?' asked Harry, his mood lifting.

'Yeah, invitation only and Mark's sorted all the

security - no phones, no filming. All set up like a charity event. We've even got some talent from local clubs doing boxing bouts. Once they're all done, we'll move 'em out before the bare knuckle bout,' said Bob, taking a gulp of his drink.

'What do the figures look like?'

Bob's big hands pulled a little notebook from his inside pocket. He thumbed through the curled-up edges before finding the page he wanted.

'We've got some big boys betting. Should clear seventy, maybe eighty grand.'

'Good work. Anything else I need to know about?' asked Harry, sliding his suit jacket off the back of the kitchen chair and moving towards the hall.

'No, Boss, we're all good,' said Bob, getting off the creaking chair and following him out the door.

Harry put his jacket on, spending the time to check his appearance in the mirror. He adjusted his collar and straightened his silk tie.

'Right. I've got an appointment with the planning office. Let's see if that greasy councillor's earned his money and got us planning permission. I'm gonna see Maureen up the hospital afterwards.'

Satisfied with his appearance Harry opened the front door.

'How's she and the boys doing?' asked Bob, filling the door on his way out.

'Not good I'm afraid. The cancer's spread. They reckon it'll be weeks rather than months. Robert seems to be holding it together ok. We don't know about

Danny; he's still in the Middle East somewhere. It'll hit him hard. It's only been a couple of years since the accident,' said Harry, suddenly standing in sombre silence.

'Well, say hello to your sister and Rob from me anyway, Boss. Tell them I'll be thinking of them.'

'Thanks, Bob. Now fuck off and get some sleep. I'll see you tonight.'

Bob nodded and walked across the crunchy gravel to his black Range Rover. He opened the door. The car rocked as he got in. Harry turned towards two black-suited men standing on the drive between the three other cars. They were heavy broad-shouldered men with wide necks and flattened noses, hand-picked by Harry and Bob from amateur boxing clubs in their youth.

'Tom, bring the Bentley round. We're going uptown,' he said before turning to the other one.

'Phil, take the Merc up the Polskis and get it cleaned for me. It looks a disgrace.'

Both men got on with their boss's instruction: you didn't keep Harry Knight waiting. The white Bentley swung round and stopped in front of him. Tom hopped out and moved around to open the passenger door. Leaving the house, the white Bentley with the HK1 number plates turned left, driving through the affluent St John's Wood, heading for the heart of London and the City of Westminster council buildings.

Stephen Taylor

BUY NOW

About the Author

Stephen Taylor was born in 1968 in Walthamstow, London.

I've always had a love of action thriller books, Lee Child's Jack Reacher and Vince Flynn's Mitch Rapp and Tom Wood's Victor. I also love action movies, Die Hard, Daniel Craig's Bond and Jason Statham in The Transporter and don't get me started on Guy Richie's Lock Stock or Snatch. The harder and faster the action the better, with a bit of humour thrown in to move it along.

The Danny Pearson series can be read in any order.

Fans of Lee Child's Jack Reacher or Vince Flynn's Mitch Rapp and Clive Cussler or Mark Dawson novels will find these book infinitely more fun. If your expecting a Dan Brown or Ian Rankin you'll probably hate them.

The Danny Pearson Thriller Series

Printed in Great Britain
by Amazon